DARK NEIGHBOURHOOD

Vanessa Onwuemezi is a writer and poet living in London. Her work has appeared in *Granta*, *Prototype*, *frieze* and *Five Dials*. Her story 'At the Heart of Things' won the White Review Short Story Prize 2019.

'I read this book with wonder and delight. Vanessa Onwuemezi is a mesmerizingly charismatic writer. Each of her stories is a mystery, an idiom, an invention.'
— Toby Litt, author of *Patience*

'In disrupted and disrupting prose, Vanessa Onwuemezi achieves the dissolution of consciousness and slippage of omniscience found in poetry and in life. Her cool authority expresses itself in rigorous, original formal decisions and a detached, exacting lyricism. The seven stories in *Dark Neighbourhood* construct our condition as a limbo in which neither the waiting nor the waited-for offers satisfaction or resolution, but in which, as the book's epigraph suggests, *Night is also a sun.*'
— Kathryn Scanlan, author of *Dominant Animal*

'Vanessa Onwuemezi's work makes legible the liminal spaces of contemporary existence: border zones at once geopolitical, metaphysical and – above all – linguistic. She sends English off on a great line of flight, from which it returns as poetry.'
— Tom McCarthy, author of *The Making of Incarnation*

'Beautiful, burning writing. The strangeness and precision of the language not only make new worlds – with a scorched poetic and political vision akin to Samuel R. Delany's best work – but bring this world into focus, in all its depravity, injustice and heartbreak.'
—Will Harris, author of *RENDANG*

Fitzcarraldo Editions

DARK NEIGHBOURHOOD

VANESSA ONWUEMEZI

CONTENTS

'Night is also a sun.'
—— Zarathustra

DARK NEIGHBOURHOOD

One bottle of water, three hundred and twenty books,
one hundred packets of cigarettes, fifty lighters, three
boxes of toothpicks, a baby bottle, five litres of whisky,
one of gin, one hundred of vinegar, six kitchen knives,
ninety tampons with applicators, ninety-five without,
a small crate of ginger ale, a box of crispy fried onions,
mismatched earrings, rings, bracelets, a love letter,
two vials of insulin, five bags of glucose, earplugs,
a month's supply of contraceptive pills, a letter of
recommendation, eight bank statements, a lemon zester,
thirty hairpins, ten syringes, a half-pint of blood.
    Now GG's got a gun and she ah   adds it to the
pile, rolls onto her backside and smokes. Later, I'll tell
you about how she dies. But for now she's smoking,
draws long into her lungs and enjoys it, like women in
advertisements enjoyed chocolate, savoured, loved,
delected, sensuated, enough of that (full stop)
    She adds it to the pile and (an ellipsis as I drift again)
the worst thing about a gunshot wound, if it doesn't kill
you right away: infection, necrosis, a body eaten away by
time   the direction of decay.
        My fingers smell metallic, touch a touch of the
barrel – it's hot, as we've been blessed this summer with
plenty of it from on high. All is lit with a blaze of shine-
yellow   so lucky, and I for one can't get enough, 'Can't
get enough of this   sunshine,' I say aloud, and the
people around me say it with me, say it all the time for
as long as the sun is with us, say it, if the heat burns you
you're alive, so say it. What else is there to do?
    In the beginning we checked our phones constantly
of course, for the time, for the news, but batteries die and
one by one the lights go out, one by one you care none

more about time, take in the sun and try to forget that your life has become a waiting, as you realize that your life was always a waiting.

Our pile is the biggest for as far as my eyes can see in daylight. The view had been obstructed by trees and hedges. Had been. Early days. Brambles stubborn are still there, to be hacked away or burned despite their bearing fruit, only to return back, hacked again. And so I see now further across the expanse and watch   people huddled amongst tree stumps which will shoot out young tendrils for the spring, which we will reduce to stumps again. Content to be among the stumps, are they? Choices. To sit at the foot of a tree stump, or a pile of books. The two choices we can make. So lucky.

GG's head a greyish cloud. And me, I sit on pile of books looking as if I have something to do. Catch sight of a gloomy figure walking towards us. Most people languish in the heat. People relaxed as anything, one of the better days. So why the gloom of this one? Closer, I recognize the shoulders sloped as an arrow – sharp, down-angled. The head shaved low. The lax chin of
friend
since the beginning
long-time friend like summoned from my
recollection, remembered figure
towards me
flush with red
face a brow dropped
reaches my books and sits
purple in worry and wrinkles
knuckles
claws at a shoe
thin sole
reveals calloused heel

14

pressed to the brake?
a graze, or bite infected
blood, clouds under skin
and breathes out   the man breathes
once
again   breathes out
and down
nose to knees and hands
pray each side of a head
broken into halves.

'Stevi, are you gonna talk?' I say.

'Leaves talk, rocks, tree stumps, the burning
fires   talk.' He scratches out that nasty heel.

'Are you tired?' I say.

'In love.'

'That your back told me as you walked away, and arm
looped into hers.'

'Long time no see.'

'Ah, some words are in the right order.'

'Help.'

'Is why you're here.'

He closes his lips, jaw tight and jowls droop. His
pride. Me, I feel no pride ever. Then from outside our
heads, high above, words ring aloud. *Love is the hardest
thing to do.* Radio tone, air shake and a flock of quiet
birds, grey striped, strange curled beaks, flee from the
shrubbery, rough ugly bark.

'Some kind of ridiculous,' Stevi says, and looks
around like casting judgement on all but unseen
fragments of dust.

Those statements, piped out at regular intervals, make
nonsense for our ears, fatherly condescension. A kind
of love, perhaps, perhaps that's it, Stevi is here, grazed,
looking rough and   in love after all.

'By the time those words reach my patch, they'll be mixed up, and some words swapped out for other words. The statement will make another sense, or another nonsense by then,' he says.

Me, breaking off a chain-thought on love, lavender coloured. 'I do feel calmer, for having heard it.'

'Yes, it is calming now you mention it. I feel better.'

'Better, yes, how awful.'

'How wretched.' He smiles a flash, and now breathing a normal pace, looks at me with eyes a syrup ready to pour. 'We want to get married.'

'Well congratulations, suck in your jowls, you look old and defeated. What's wrong then?'

'A ring   lost.'

'There's the problem out, and what do you want from me?'

'I had wondered if (a pause and again, a pause) it might have come to you.'

Smart, objects seem to reach me eventually. Even if I'm fourth in the chain of digestion, at some point or another it's in my pile.

'GG keeps the inventory,' I say.

She's curled up asleep with her favourite rough blanket and pillow – we the ones with luxuries – the cigarette, half-burned, lies beneath her open mouth. Her hair is gold, as applies to hair and not the gold of a ring (comma, another thought) or that which might be painted on a cheap picture frame, as well as the grey of pencil shaded across paper lightly striping her head. Mine is black as far as I know, only see it when I'm pulling it out.

'Let's look, we might get lucky.'

'So lucky,' he says, the words sound flat coming out of his mouth.

We look through the jewellery, disorganized on shelves. Some earrings I get as ones and some in twos. Rings, there are many, but some are cheap and some not so. GG's better at telling the difference. With the jewellery, I keep other metals, brass knuckles I acquired not long ago, in exchange for insulin, insulin given for a clean pair of socks, which I had gotten in bulk after an accident, they needed blood, pills for pain and bandages – cloth for cloth – plaster of Paris I threw in at no extra cost, good business, my list at the beginning was not exhaustive. And all this   stuff, the descendants of a single earring, given in exchange for a packet of nuts because she was hungry and I, missing my earring, was hungry to feel like myself again.

I amassed objects and traded them for things others would give up in exchange for something they wanted more. I've a talent for understanding value, to feel safe, for example, much value in that, such a feeling could be sold with anything. The brass knuckles, or some bullshit crystals, a newspaper – very common, with a crossword, even better. I once traded back a grandmother's necklace to a girl who had lost a tooth after she parted with it, bad luck   so she said, so she believed. And she'd rather have had the necklace to eating that day, that week, so I ate.

'And the ring, how does it look?' Eyes strain from scanning up and down.

'Um   looks like someone should wear it while engaged.'

'You're much help. I'd forgotten you, Stevi.'

'I know,' he says. His eyes trace a bewildered circle around the stock, and then, 'Yes!'

'It's this?' An emerald with silver band.

'Yes, it's this.' He sighs, 'Thank you, old friend.'

But I know that his quivering eyes, his tightened jaw, are trying their best to hide a lie. As if   he could have ever gotten himself a ring to lose.

'Love is safe again,' I say to this old friend, 'I need to piss, I'll walk you some of the way back.' I make a gesture to GG, woken by our rifling, 'A piss.'

She nods and sits up to look alert. Now, it's easier   some, to leave GG alone for time longer than I could have before. The gun, some protection for the stock and to keep my place in line, allows me to dig a deeper groove in time, right now, for myself and Stevi.

To the waste pit, human waste, though it's more like a heap than a pit, animals give it a wide berth and the people who run it now are much worse than the last. They like it for entertainment, sadistic, but you can scarcely waste anywhere else now, anywhere else is only where you yourself sleep and eat, or someone else who will kill you for wasting where they lay themselves down. I pay for both of us – walnuts in shell – and as we enter, at the start of a forking path, we see a young woman washing down a child's thin limbs, skin so tight to the bone, sallow.

'Wash him somewhere else young lady,' Stevi says to her, 'not in this festering mess, you idiot.'

He looks at me, avoiding her eyes as we pass.

'Nice to know you haven't changed, Stevi.'

'And you,' he says, and pats the pocket transporting the ring to his beloved.

With that I grab him by the neck and jowl, and rub his face for a while in the piss. I'd first thought of shit, but with that it's much harder to keep your own hands clean.

And during I say, 'Old friend
to love
is the hardest thing

18

do your best
to think lavender thoughts.'

I take another route towards the exit. We must
accommodate this mess by walking orderly, in one
direction. I would usually take some things with me to
trade on a trip like this, economizing. In this spot there
are many young children, I'd put on a friendly smile
and say, 'Children's books? Toy cars? Dolls, stickers
and fizzy sweets?' And more rarely, 'Computer games?'
Today, my anger eclipses my good sense. Stevi, his face
in the piss, the ring I threw into the dirt, he can look for
it as love is love must be worth it.

Emerged from the labyrinth dung-heap, I walk back
to my pile, passing the line of waiting people. Whispers
of the last statement from the gate still bounce from
mouth to mouth, just as the words had bounced around
my mind. Can't blame us. What else is there to think
or speak? The people here say, 'Love is hard', that
much has arrived undistorted. But then, as Stevi says,
the statement morphs, and interpretation is anyone's
to make, 'Love is a hard shell that must be cracked',
'Love is done and must be buried', and a few kilometres
further away, and away and away, it becomes something
like, 'Bury your loved ones.' All from a single source
(comma) who? The god from the gate?

There are floodlights high above us, illuminated both
day and night erase the moon, intensify the sun. No child
born here will ever know the moon waxing, or its smile
that wanes to a slither of silver, new moon, the cold half-
moon. To live in a world filled with light is like being
slowly erased. No longer knowing down or up, yes or no,
day a true night. Light upon light is darkness.

The first time I heard the gate speak, human voice

crackling through speaker system, it seemed genuine as we rapped our fists on metal door of it. 'It' that had appeared this day I mention, blocking our path on a cold walk home. *I have a good friend in your position*, it said. *Nobody should have to go through what you're going through*, it said. *We take your concerns very seriously*. I asked it to be specific, 'Who is this friend? And what happens to them next?' shouting in the direction of the speaker, but a man next to me (open bracket) who had all his teeth, whose breath was mint fresh, who was a 'smart casual' dresser, and spoke well, with an accent more trustworthy than most including my own (close bracket) explained to me that this empathy should be considered sincere, and that we should be reasonable people and wait.

I had no words for the dense feeling in my stomach, it didn't deserve expression just then. I decided to sit and rest in place, amongst a crowd of people trapped on the path that came to be known as the way through, and we remained reasonable people, as the next hundred, then thousand people bedded down in following nights, as the first trees were felled for firewood, the first tooth was pulled, a baby was born, gunshot fired. Yes   is my answer to all that, and still a yes I rest in place, bathed in the hellish acid-lemonade, watching my head roll over the moving sky, in this eternal waiting room only one magazine to be found. Our salvation on the other side of the gate seems assured, we hear long cries of bliss from over there that say, 'Hold on just a few days more.'

There, vague history of how I came to be stationary one day on this space of tarmac.

Back at my pile my world at my feet, eat an apple, bread roll, drink of water and vodka, bite of warm cucumber. The well-dressed man I never saw again and assumed, being so reasonable, that he had passed through the gate and was taking the everlasting sip of bliss. Whatever he held most dear in his mind would have been given to him – that is what we've been promised, the gate keeps our spirits up, goads us on to want in myriad ways, for us to interpret and reinterpret our own most original wants. Of the first people to find themselves trapped here only a few remain nearby. GG is one, fills my eyes the biggest (full stop)

The space behind us is occupied by a young woman, a layabout, which says something when there's not much to do but just that. Savina – the name, not that I use it much. She's a friend of GG's and I just about tolerate her edging around my space. She's tried to help in the past, to sell, proven herself a burden. Spends a lot of time flossing her teeth and wondering aloud whether she's doing it enough. Right now in my eye-corner, head lolling between her knees, then snapping upright with wide eyes a stare that doesn't meet any other eyes. I don't ask what she's been up to.

'We're missing some stock,' says GG.

'Nothing gets past you   eh,' I say, 'nothing.'

'Nothing as long as nothing is past.'

'I'm lost.'

'I know.'

'I gave the ring to Stevi, strike it off.'

'Done. But there's more.' GG flicks a pencil over the list.

'What more?' I say.

'Two gin, ten newspapers and some hair,' she says, without blinking.

'Were you asleep?' Hand curls to a fist.

'Not asleep, of course not asleep. But there was only me, you spent a long time pissing.' No response from

21

me, she adds – a saying – 'For the want of a nail the shoe was lost.'

I amassed the stuff without stealing it. To be robbed, injustice, an energizing feeling, energized to keep order and fairness around my patch, by the radius of a gunshot's reach, at least. So we put the gun to good use, I hook it to the front of my trousers, and stand on top of pile every morning pressing out my hips it's all on show, and GG takes the afternoon shift to say – without having to say – to a potential thief, Think twice arsehole, think twice.

Watching GG up there I say, 'Is the safety on?'

'The what?' she says.

'The safety.'

'What's that?'

'I've heard it in films, when the character is holding a gun they don't want to fire they say about the safety.'

'Dunno what that's about. Let's hope,' she says, and puts her hands on her hips.

The gate is painted black, steel is the metal most likely, in sheets bolted flush, layers of paint flake away to reveal yet more layers of black. We stand most of the time facing the gate, and we sleep with heads pointing towards the gate, always looking ahead at the gate   closed. Me, in the beginning, slept too long and lost my first place in line, my fault, fortunes always rising and falling this way, conniving my way up again has been my strategy, and the line moves, it does, because people disappear from the front, quietly to avoid a stampede, reasonable people. With GG here, we as two both better off. Stevi was up here with me at the beginning, near, much nearer to the gate, but he fell into love (full stop)

Rest in place, pass through in good time.

On the tail-end of these words   I hear   water-drop of pennies falling onto tarmac. GG's ears twitch. A wrestle is getting started, and for this, the gate's advice is also dropped to the ground for the sake of entertainment; a piece of something to watch, jeer at, laugh us out of restlessness.

'Come!' I say to Savina, 'Hold this bag.' An easy job that even she can do.

GG's already up ahead, with a bag of pennies for exchange (dash) 'pennies' a name for small change, buttons, nuts, hairpins. The one or two gathering into a crowd barter with us, buy, and throw their pennies at the feet of the wrestlers – the only way to solve an argument, once reason is spent, and the pennies go to the loser as their place in line will likely be lost. A petty fight over a girl? An idea? As if anything is as serious, could be more serious than the gate, so dark and impenetrable and this   is bright, their skin luminous with sweat. As the pennies fall they roll along the wandering paths of our minds, as we escape briefly the command to *Rest in place*, the desires that keep us up at night – to be on the other side of the gate, to rest asleep next to some body, exuder of warmth, and the cry of bliss to be more than a constant ringing in my ears, but my body's scream.

The slip of skin over skin, the pound of feet on the ground and 'Yeeeeah', everyone has picked a side, one of the wrestlers has no friends here. Thump of back on the ground and I feel my own back, the wince of graze and blood of fresh-opened skin as the two have out the last throes. No shelter from the stares of us, or the advancing brow of clouds whose darkened sagging centres release a drop and   a drop.

Hold out your hand and feel it wet. Marks the end of

the sunshine then, as seasons turn us over.

Five, six, seven, eight, nine, ten, a winner!

And loser lies next to a spray of pennies and breathing heavily through a mess of hair, open-mouthed, letting in the rain.

We scatter. With a bag of stuff marginally better than the pennies we traded: some cigarettes half-smoked, not bad, little candles, better. Split between the three of us. And now the challenge to keep it dry. Looking at the shuddering sheets of water, I remember a film I once saw: a boat sails through a valley of waves, plunged and rising, side to side, the sea has a human face, mouth gaping to swallow the boat and its crew, their mouths open and screaming. An omen, because the rain only heavies. The whole area is flooding.

'We cut down all the trees,' Savina moans, sitting on a wooden palette.

GG and I gather up what we can.

'What first?' GG says.

I freeze. What's worth saving? It depends on who is wanting, what is given in exchange, the level of desperation, rainfall, whether my stomach is rumbling, how much sleep I've had. The need of a person is one aspect, their wants are a complex thing. I don't know. GG takes charge as my thoughts wear a hole in my head.

We hike up the newspapers and foodstuffs, bandages and alcohol, cigarettes, bags of blood, make-up and lotions, children's books, used diaries and notebooks, hair cuttings and blankets, tie them high with rope. We both stand on top of books piled, arranged with the most literary and those in foreign languages on the bottom. Keep our feet dry.

Savina is right, the drenching floods only began after the trees were cut. The waste heap, in the distance, is

24

slipping away like a melting block of ice. The gun handle
hangs precariously from GG's slack pocket. There is
more stock missing, she says to me from her perch, we
left it unguarded too long. Why so much theft, all of a
sudden? I say. It's likely to be one or two people at a time,
she tells me, things disappearing in small numbers. Most
of the people here, I had thought, were decent people.
But I see that things are turning for the worse.

We wait
the rain   cling like I'm
pelted with spit
in disgust I'm angry
are all emotions this quick?

Don't think for yourselves, we can think for you.
I'm thinking, thinking. I'm reasonable, responsible.
Haven't learned my neighbours' names   oh   but
they change so quickly. And who among them is
leeching off us? GG and I have the staying power,
we the high achievers. They   relaxed as anything,
languishing in sewage sludge now they habituate to it
squelching between their toes. Luckier ones sitting on
the tree stumps, listening for the sound of the lost forest,
laughing at us.

Wrestler still lying on his back as the rain tapers off.
Alive? Yes, in soaked clothes and hair, washed of sweat
and blood (comma) though some blood still lodged
in the corners of his mouth. He rises, crawls, searches
for his pennies in lagoons of rain and waste, retching
from the stench. He sits his arse on a wooden box, feet
submerged in sludge, opens his mouth, belly distends
and a dry moan emerges from his throat, the animal in
him. That crucial part of our longing, after a flood, is
revitalized in some of us as a weed, rooted deeper into

hope, and for others it is washed away leaving a hopeless void, a moan from a parched throat.

I don't wait for my feet to touch dry ground before setting traps with powder-paint as thief identifier, alarms with bells and mousetraps. GG is watching me with an amused look.

'We'll starve to death without stuff to sell, you know. I'm the only one who thinks ahead,' I say with the force of my stomach.

'No disapprove here. Nothing said, see.' Her hands are raised.

'Then help!' I say.

'I'm in my post, aren't I?' She has gun on show, hips out, the stance that says think twice. I take over from her, we haven't stopped, even during the flood. You have to work hard to assert a new order of things. She sorts through the jewellery, counting, jotting things down in pencil. She picks up a ring, takes off a shoe, loops the ring over her second toe and stretches out her foot. I give attention, how she balances on one foot and gazes at her toe. She seems to be here and not here, has some way of existing amongst the mess which takes her out of it (dash) I'm distracted, jut my hips out and look around.

'What were you doing before you got here?' GG says, puncturing the relative quiet.

'You know we've always been here.'

'That's not true.' The foot is tucked beneath her now, sitting she looks at me. 'Me, I travelled. I've been to Lithuania. There, I heard a saying, "It is good fishing in troubled waters." '

'Ooooh,' Savina says, with her nose in our conversation. 'I've never travelled. Epping, I went there once.'

'You?' GG says to me.

'I've been to Cuba.' GG looks at me intently, drawing more out, drawing blood. 'There, they have a saying, "No hay santo sin muerto."'

'What does it mean?' Savina says.

'I wouldn't know.' I check the gun is still in place.

'You don't speak any Spanish?' she says.

'I do ah I did.'

'Well there it is,' she laughs in a way that feels like a scratch on the inside of my throat. I tell her to shut up and take gun in my hand, only loosely. But they overreact, Savina cowers on her palette and GG grabs my arm.

'I'm not insane, I wouldn't shoot her just for that. But I'd love to scare her away.' That puts an end to the talk. Savina turns her back, good. GG and I wait long into the following days for stagnant water to thicken to scum.

Hold in your mind your dear ones, the gate.

'My dear ones,' Neighbour just ahead of me says and caps his mouth after the blurt. Then he says hello to me for the first time. We wave hands across the strand of scum, the ground between us.

We've spoken for transaction before. But this hello has a lonely timbre, has more the ring of something human. I say hello
    lips crack as my mouth stretches for the word
    I am parched
    suspicious
    and tempting to be
    drinking handfuls
    the look of rainwater
    deepens thirst
    my body
    washed back to the animal

my head urges to wander
towards the sound of the
moaning
ones, given up
on the wait.

'A long wait?' he says. I see that he is toothless but for three in his gum, hanging on.

'Something like that,' I say.

'Something like that,' GG says, I didn't know she was paying attention, smoking, her eyes looking out with soft gaze.

'What's it all for?' he says.

I wince. We're not supposed to ask ourselves that, questions play havoc with everything, and when we're so close to the gate.

His mouth runs from him, 'My family – partner and child – I want them back, the year when it was good.'

'Bold. To say it, I mean.'

'I'm helpless to say it.' His gaze presses on something indefinite.

'I'm waiting for the truth.' Another voice, who's she? Sitting on stump like it's a floating barrel. Body small enough to tuck in her feet. 'Truth, on its own, the purest thing to want.'

'Truth is a woman,' says GG, 'the form of a woman, pale, nude, with nipples almost the same colour as the rest of her skin.'

'No, brown nipples,' voices now from forward and back, 'brown is the colour of the earth, of nature, and her lips are roses, that grow from the earth, from a bush, don't forget.'

'Yes,' says GG, fickle in her ideas, 'the breast is melon-shaped, of course, melons grow on a vine close to the earth, did you know that? The vine grows flat at first, then curls in the sun.' Her outstretched hand enacts her speech. 'And the melon nestles on the earth   uh huh like the breast of woman, on her chest.'

Earthborn, brown nipples. Now I've heard it all.

I must be close to the end now?

Surely now.

On the other side of the gate there are arms waiting to embrace me, legs ready to part for me. I don't know who she is, but I'm sure that she is Love.

The discussion breaks off into details of this woman of truth – her hands, her fingernails, the texture of her hair. Then with the ground still scummy we unpack some stock as people, weathering the stench, come looking for their usual distractions. After-flood comforts are selling well: cigarettes, porn, gas canisters and tinned food.

Savina and GG break in work and speak of things women speak of, passing the gun back and forth.

'Would you blow your brains out to lose three pounds?' Savina says, and holds the thing to her temple.

'Don't, you idiot, you don't know how to use a gun,' GG says.

'I know more than you think,' Savina waves it around her head.

GG makes a grab and it fires. And people around the scene   some throw themselves to the ground, some run, some as if nothing happened. And GG, the bullet leaves a wound like a ditch, deep in her outer thigh.

'Not too much harm done,' she says, as we barely stem the blood soaking through her trousers.

'Not much,' I say.

The next period of time is so drawn out that it deserves its own heading.

¶ The Slow Death of GG

Deaths are permissible when there is no hope.

Her thigh plugged, with a poultice of moss, cotton soaked in disinfectant, and bandage wrapped tight no longer bleeds. But it has failed to heal for too long. Now watching her shiver with pain and the leg red hot.

Neighbour – 'my dear ones' – is useful, and helps to keep my stock moving, for a commission, and wraps and re-wraps the bandages like he's done it before and before. He feeds her drinks with vitamins, and cigarettes. I feed her with talk of her woman of truth, reassuring her that she will find her, growing of this   melon vine, succulent full of water, nature seed and propagation, newness. I know it, I tell her. She smiles weakly, I see them lifted, the corners of her mouth.

'You think I'm fickle in my ideas, don't you,' she says. And she tells me that it doesn't matter what form Truth takes, as long as you find it. She reminds me that it was her who taught me sayings such as, 'The squeaky wheel gets the grease,' 'The enemy of my enemy is my friend' and 'The right tools for the right job.' These sayings we have lived by to survive.

Neighbour asks me to look through my pile for medicine. Lifting up the bandages to look at GG's wound, he shakes his head, 'Infected.'

I find the medicine, shelved next to a red Russian doll.

'Antibiotics, as you asked.' I hand him a small bottle with tight cap.

'These will do.'

I breathe deep and lean over GG.

'Where do you get these things from?' he says, still looking at the red-and-blue wound and not at me.

'Well   uh   people ask for things and I give them

those things, in exchange for something else, and I accumulate.'

'But your supply, how'd you come across all these books newspapers antibiotics porn magazines and cigarettes? Where does it begin? Must be some place outside as the rest of us have nothing.'

The question pierces the skin of sense I've wrapped over this whole endless duration, all duration, waiting here.

'So we rub it on?' I say, about the antibiotics.

'No, Jesus.' He opens the cap, gets her to swallow.

Where does it all come from? I've never asked. Perhaps the line has grown so much now, the whole world is here. Hopeless to think that all of them might pass through one day soon. Stock is still disappearing, now even I can see it without GG having to tell me. But I'm so close to the gate, I tell myself, it will be my time in not too long.

He shows me a piece of paper, a line twisting through a valley of little stars, dotted over the whole thing, except in certain patches.

'A map,' he says.

'What are these stars?' I say.

He says that they're the lights of people.

'And there are no people here?' I point at the empty patches.

'Yes, there are people,' he says, but those neighbourhoods are dark.

'No lights there?'

'No light to see.'

'Black?'

'Deeper than black,' he says, 'impossible to avoid them, only know that you're in one when it's dark – forward, sideways and back.'

'And the people wait in the dark?'

'Their voices descend on you,' he says, his eyes two lumps of coal. 'A sound like   cacophony of beetles crawling over each other, clicking armours, exoskeletons. But listen careful and you'll hear that it's the echoes of their thoughts. It's too easy to follow a thought deeper deep into darkness. I was lost a long time.'

'I could sell them torches, batteries, or candles.'

'No point. No bodies, heads or torsos, only the glint-flash of teeth and eyes. Illusions. They're thoughts, only thoughts. When I ran I touched no body, and nobody touched me. Only the thoughts that followed me out.' He sucks his thumb.

Never thought of mapping the place. Not worth the effort. To what end? Too risky to leave the line for long, people get ideas, conspire to eject others for their own benefit. No word of these neighbourhoods so far, no news gets out, only those rogue thoughts, corrupting whispers, undermining, like Neighbour with his questions thinks too much, and now I know why, because of where he's been.

'Brave, to travel so much, you might have lost your place, been sent to the end, wherever that is,' I say.

'You've not travelled?'

'I have, to some places I remember. To Moscow.'

'Ah Moscow, never been, but I've been to Sorrow.'

'A feeling.'

'What?'

'Sorrow is a feeling, not somewhere to go. Perhaps you meant Glasgow? Was it raining?'

'No, there was sunshine.'

'Morocco? How did you get there?'

'I found myself there. I'm sure it was Sorrow, a long

flat coast, and a flatter sea.'

'Sounds okay then.'

'And why do some wait, those who don't even have
the end in sight?' He elbows towards the gate, which is
becoming more active. When it isn't repeating its last
statement, it is mumbling whispers.

We turn heads towards it, to hear more closely, in
the hope that it will shout out the go-ahead, for us to
get up and move through it   open. I try to answer his
question, though I feel sick.

'It's reasonable to think
all people   to
pass through the gate
in good time.'

grit behind my eyes
scratch of fingernail
the catch, my teeth
twist I bite it off

the mind will bend
until it breaks.

Wandering around the pile where   I try   to trace the
route of each object valued and traded for an ask (full
stop) Impossible. My eye draws back to the Russian doll,
looks like one I used to have.

In Moscow. I was passing the days wandering the
halls of a gigantic hotel, casino on the ground floor, tried
my luck and lost. And corridor after long corridor, in
midnight blue, each door uniform in red, but for the
numbers, gold. I didn't care to ask anyone the way to
the canteen, but found a gift shop, bought the doll and
took her out on the town. To the chapel, sermon today

is in Russian, as every day, knees to the altar, and GG interjects, 'I've no chance of a climax if you don't touch me down there,' puts her finger on her cheek and twists, she's wearing a dress of burlap, and her hair is short green grass. Then, the canteen, the lights too bright, walls of turquoise or cerulean, and pork, salted egg, the curdled white of GG's eyes.

It's worse than I thought, of course it is.

Her nose is singing the wind as she sleeps. She's drowsy hard to wake, covered with sweat. Look at the wound, Neighbour says, it's black and green, and she's hot to the touch.

The sun will not rise, seems to have abandoned us finally. The floodlight the only sun now, but it bathes everything in a light so harsh, I fear other people.

Think freedom and be free.

'My dear ones,' Neighbour says again to nobody. Twisting a dirty bandage between two fists, disgusting. He's looking at me now. Put it down, the filth, wash your hands before touching anything – my look says it without my mouth needing to open. He obeys, bucket of water and soap, whistles cheerfully through three teeth while he scrubs between fingers.

I would cut him open, drain his blood to swap for GG's. If I knew how.

She mustn't die.

Now she's moaning quietly, delirious, her mouth open glistening red. I am in pain, she says, and I say it with her, and put into her mouth a lit cigarette. People come to buy but I'm too off   to sell. No thought makes sense, they only pour as a stream from my nose.

I lie down next to her with a pen in my hand, and I'm ordered onto my knees to fill in the missing punctuation

of this long scroll. Yellowed edges and musty of old.
Pen a nightmare to operate but I must: full stop, colon,
semi-colon, speech mark, open bracket and close
bracket, forward slash, comma, exclamation mark,
question mark, apostrophe, dash, quotation mark and
every error sends me to the beginning again. Mark after
mark, endless and I feel it, every moment of it. My mind
is dragging somewhere behind me.

The cigarette burns down and she's green   gone.

The solution is elsewhere.

Neighbour stands, and behind him (comma) guilty,
Savina. I toss him aside and her   I hit, as nameless
bystanders pile in. Oh   can't hit a woman, can't hit her
on the side of her face, can't bust her lip that curls over
dumb as a wet rose, can't kick her in the head as I just
did, can't stamp on her hand to finish as I'm dragged off.

'You do things others wouldn't to get all this stuff,'
she says. Revealed as a thief, no surprise, jewellery and
tampons strewn on the ground about her. I make a grab
for her again but am blocked, need some salve to apply
to the anger, shapeless wound.

'I never steal or kill,' I say.

We never steal or kill, they all say back to me, and
they chorus aloud the shit we've swallowed (colon)

about reasonability
and responsibilities of people
for one another and
unreasonable to
hit a woman
and
not her fault
and terrible accident
and you have all

the antibiotics anyway
brotherhood
sisterhood, freedom
togetherness for
we
will pass through
in good time.

My clenched fist blooms to a hand and I say to
Neighbour, 'We'll wrap her up, in burlap, and spread
wax on her eyes to keep them closed for now.'

'For you,' he says and hands me a knife. I cut off GG's
hair, hard to find kindling these days. We wrap her in
burlap and I insist   alone   scoop up the body and
carry her through the gathered nameless crowd. Grey
faces sink into atmosphere's soup. Some guilty part of
myself I need to cut out and they   look around me and
through me as I walk five kilometres back.

As I pass, even young children know not to look
at GG's limp feet, tuft of hair from the roll of burlap I
carry, some superstition that death is contagious, and
they are already tainted by guilt and violence in thoughts
and   nowhere to bury her but the trash heap with the
others, in the part of the forest that's left, without sun
grows a frost, the ground too hard to dig.

I take this body and I   be alone with it. Us
concealed by the stronghold of trees, a narrow avenue
where her body will have improper burial.

Is this about love? Yes it is, always.

Love of the woman I crave, she could have been the
one who's now dead at my feet.

There's less of the floodlight here and it's a rare place
empty of people, damp earth a comfort to my nose,
real darkness in the shadowed parts. Cobwebs catch
the light, GG had called them 'spider spit'. She's green,

I could lie down and take pleasure in her, take off my shoes and walk over her easy as a green afternoon. I'm alone with her and want to make love, but nothing down there stirs.

'My love,' I say, to no one in particular.

Walking back, I see that her outline has contoured itself to my vision. Her curves, the bend of the path as I leave the forest and follow it home to my space in line, fingers in the gnarled roots pushing through the tarmac, her knees tree stumps, the swirling juice of my thoughts stirred by her rotating hips, and lungs the breath of smoke rising from the burning fires, her climax. The blank of her mind, the gate.

Imagine the shape of the line from above. It will look like a meandering river, sprawling in places, snake with belly full. A shape with no predestination as person after person lays their body down to wait here for a mindless amount of time. You'll see that some neighbourhoods are dotted with tiny lights from fires or electricity. And others are completely dark. Not even an arm or leg outstretched. No glint of an iris looking. No taut skin-enveloped bodies' glow and shadow of youth. Illusions, floating in dark, that's all.

I have sight of my pile. Neighbour rests his elbow on crate of soda water, waves at me bright-eyed as I approach, as if nothing that happened before has happened.

'The gate spoke.'

'And so?'

'*Have a safe journey*, it said, and cracked open a little, you see?'

I see nothing, it looks just as before. But there are noises coming from the speaker, creaking of metal, groaning of rivets awakening, shedding their rust. Around me people pack up their scarce belongings, scooping up those old newspapers bought from me, hairpins and old bracelets, medicines, hats and scarves, badges, pins, baby bottles.

I look at the pile I built, with GG.

'Leave it,' Neighbour says, as I run my hands over books and jars of jam, the gun, brass knuckles and nail clippers.

'I'll take some of it,' I say.

People are moving towards the gate, they must be getting through. I pick up a bag and fill it, with what, who knows. I don't know the value of a thing.

'Leave it,' he says again, with insistence, and then further away, 'it's nothing now that we're gone.'

I hook the bag over my shoulder and move urgent, like pulled by a thread tied to my tooth. The bag slips from me, but crowd's momentum lifts me, moving me forwards, hear my things crunch underfoot, and then as a distant rattle.

The wind will enjoy rattling through those objects now we're gone. A bottleneck at the gate squeezes the gathering crowd to a crush, shoulder to shoulder my toes just about on the ground. And through my body rushes the heat generated by all of us pushed together. In front, I see the gate wide open, deep cavern of mouth. And no elation on the approach, as I've always expected, because on the other side of the gate I see nothing but my own eyes staring back. The advance is endless, as if the whole duration of our suffering here is re-played, moment by moment, each step we take. I   embedded in mass of people legs and arms bonded, twisted together, bodies and faces lost to the want. Except for the eyes. And I wonder if anyone else can see this, if they too can see their own eyes staring back at them from beyond the gate. GG, I'm a fool, I say to myself, but I don't say it aloud. Compelled I keep marching forwards on my toes in this endless advance that goes nowhere, and I ask myself why we can't turn around, why we never turned around to look for some other way through. Why us starved people have been waiting, wanting hopeless wants and are now running towards them in the night as a sea of heads. Silence has fallen on us, no cries of bliss, all is covered in a layer of hush as we dampen down, a fog hanging low. And I look around at the other people, at the backs and sides of their heads, while they are staring straight ahead   only ahead.

CUBA

Policeman walks towards her, gun swinging from his
hip, cracked stones rolling beneath his feet, head lifted
high by some   vapours which only he can sense in cold
blue air. Moves as if he's standing still and it's the earth
that aids him, aids him forward.

His uniform is olive green, gun hovers by her open
window, a hand on the roof and all is still, the birds hold
their breath while she feels the engine vibrating through
her seat.

'Buenos días, señora,' he says.

'That for cracking coconuts?' she says to the gun.

He laughs, then a gesture with the hand.

Now she stands, leaning against the car warms her
thigh, grey smoke as the engine burns a veil to cloak her
mouth and nose, while she flirts with tired eyes, body
soaked in this morning's sweat, the dew, gathered as she
passed through border after border on this long drive.

He looks at the exhaust, the smoke. 'Oil,' he says.

'Okay,' she says.

'Your name?' He leans himself against the car, clink of
the gun.

'Cuba.' A lie.

True enough to her, grown up breathing the vapours
of a place she's never been

Cuba   edging round the fields.

Cuba, rubbing its   legs together from the long grass.

Cuba, dripping warm from her eyelashes as she steps
out of rain later that morning, into a hotel, in a coastline
Spanish town.

The hotel is pink all over, as the bitten inside of her
mouth, as her dark father's radiant bottom lip, as the

scar stretching down the back of her mami's calf   then there's an oil lamp burning, a blackened ceiling, the baby's head wet with tears.

'The hotel was white,' says the receptionist, 'but it wanted to be pink.' He smiles, hands her the keycard, 'Fifth floor.'

Behind him, another receptionist shuffles quiet feet, trying to catch a mosquito in a jar, 'Coño,' his mouth not so quiet, 'I don't like to kill.'

She loops her bag handles over her arm, slip   down to her elbow along hairs wet with rain. The arm aches under the weight.

Smoking on the terrace, she ignores the English man sitting easy with tall glass in hand, legs outstretched, like a grassy bank rolling into sand into a cold sea. The terrace is framed by hotel room windows set into the flesh of the walls, meekly dressed in greyed netting. The terrace wants a pool or a fountain, something to draw the eye. Any noise echoes from the walls like the click-ripple of a stone into water.

His glass finds its way to her table, the sound of metal dragging over the tiles and he says cigarette? She doesn't answer, but looks up into his red-stained eyes and hands him the one in her mouth.

'Can't get enough of this   sunshine.' He inhales.

Her ear starts ringing and she's deafened on one side for a moment. Views his mouth slightly parted, dumbly. Cracked fingernails. Hair falls wiry around his ears and nearly to his shoulders, sips his beer, foam gathers to a drop of milk and hangs from his bottom lip. He's young, from the way he talks, but looking as if each year has doubled up on his face, his back hunched like stem of yellow flower drooping. He's been here a while, he says to her, looking out for himself, left the business he started under the care of a friend. He lies, she can taste it. He touches her arm too many times. The cigarette smoke reminds her of the car and the two dogs she saw hanging from a tree by the road.

Excuses, makes her excuses and leaves.

In her room, Mami is sitting on the edge of the bed holding an unlit cigarette, staring at the wall. She was never a smoker. 'When will you let me go?' she says. She's been moving things around. On the table in the corner, white plastic cups of water in a circle, Cuba walks over to look at her own warped face – eye, half-mouth, chin.

She scours online for a job and a new place to stay, '6 May, agency staff required', and a number to call.

The agency calls her back that afternoon. And a day after that, she's handed a maid's uniform and a keycard in a room beneath some stairs, open the door and in comes the frantic reflection of light from a swimming pool, chlorine and waft of blossom, while flies, not yet lazied by the stretch of summer, rush in and out again.

He had eyed her figure for her dress size, lingering over her stomach, down to her legs. She pulls at her shirt, tight over her belly. A ball of heat familiar burns down her throat, to work its way through her and lodge itself somewhere. Good. As long as it's somewhere hidden, it's all good.

'You're staying where?'

'Manolo Hotel, for now.'

'You're looking?'

'Sí.'

'There's a board.' He points at a large square on the wall across the room, above a worn sofa, paper notices.

She nods.

'Come from?'

'U.K.,' she says.

'Where else?'

'Y soy Cubana.'

He walks over to a locker and taps it with his middle finger, reaches inside his pocket, pulls out a padlock and keys which he throws in her direction. She holds out a hand and watches the metal crash onto floor tiles. A crescent echo lingers in the air, in an arc from his hand to the floor. She sees it. Just as she sometimes observes the moon separated out into image after image, tracking its movement across the sky   frame frame of the moon. At the same time, in her ear, the low croak of frogs mating at night.

'Be careful!' He steps into sunlight coming through the door. Two illumined grey hairs in his moustache. 'I won't give you another.' Sucks his teeth.

A knock at the door, weak as the crack of paper. A blonde woman stands in the doorway, dressed for work.

'Noda,' he introduces. At Noda's feet a fly crawls a centimetre along the floor   stops.

'You ready?' she says to Cuba, who nods.

Noda leads her up a floor and explains, mouth running quick Spanish, taps her finger on the coloured lids of plastic containers, spray bottles, cloths, towels, plastics, bedding, on a trolley outside of room 166. 'You're supposed to use this cloth for the dirty stuff, everywhere a normal person would put their ass. This one for everywhere else in the bathroom.'

Cuba's mouth searches for words in Spanish, hasn't spoken it in a long while, strains her mind forehead tightens, later, rubs her temples on the bus home.

In the room, she un-makes the bed while Noda

watches, between opening the curtains, emptying bins.

'Not bad, but you'll have to speed up. You'll have all this floor and another to do. We cut corners.' She takes a sheet between two fingers and laughs a bottomless laugh, while miming a scissor motion. She shows Cuba how to fold the corners beneath the mattress, pull it taut, tuck it under, pulls it all out and makes her start again, hair now in wisps around her neck as they hold between their fingers the quivering white.

A studio apartment, eighth floor, facing a wall on one side. The light dim it feels like she's half-sunk into the ground. On the other side, in the distance she can see a square, the plaza. The kitchen is tidied away in a cubby with a small table, where she puts a little bottle of rum she found in a hotel room, and two chairs. 'Oye, tú qué haces aquí?' she hears Mami say, the voice mixing into the smell of plantain and beans, cucumbers long as cold running water, dusted with black pepper, and avocado felt up with a palm and five fingers for it to be hard and soft enough, to be ripe. Mami stands next to the kitchen table, pulling plates filled with food out of her shirt and dropping them heavy, she's angry, picks up a tea towel and curses, 'Cabrona, no te metas conmigo.' Whip-snaps it in the air.

Suitcase unpacked, Cuba stares out of the window towards the plaza, a stone stretched flat under the sun, light pushing away shadow to its edges. Mami stands nearby, calmer, the remembered smells still emanating from her. She's mouthing words as if in prayer, her lips feeling their way around a song from an old tale, isé kué, ariyénye, isé kué, ariyénye, isé kué, ariyénye, isé kué, ariyénye, droning as she watches people walk past down below, sloughing off the colours of their tanned feet and

leaving it all to melt on the pavement slabs   brown,
window cracked a little, wafting in the brown of skin.

With a square of burlap and purple cloth, Cuba tries
to create from memory something she lost. Stones,
shells, herbs, anise, all tied up with string. Mami had
been a santera, priestess, a good one, had made her
a charm tied with seven knots of string to ward off
bad spirit. A charm, a desire, so slow to bend things,
powerful and slow like water cutting through stone.

She folds and unfolds her bed sheets, getting better at
smoothing out the creases with a slick hand. She knocks
a breast and gasps, cups it, breast sore, full engorged,
takes off her bra and squeezes.

Down in the plaza she lights a cigarette while her ass
finds a chair and sits, winces at the heat of metal, a hot
egg rolling under her thigh. She goes walking with the
cigarette burning between her fingers, finds a museum,
looks into a crypt from the top of the stairs, walls the red
of clay, graves gaping open like a mouth of pulled teeth.
Alone, she goes inside and waits a while in the cool,
saying her own name out loud to the bones and clean
smiling skulls.

Looping around to the port, she walks through
drowsy streets with regular palm trees that droop
towards her as she passes, shrubs bursting with pink
blossom, lawns, behind them hills like dusty mounds, all
a faded rush of grass with no beckoning. No promise.

A dog edges over and sits beside her while she's
stopped to look, scratches its snout and follows in her
shadow as she moves on, dipping its nose to the ground
every once in a while like a shishi odoshi, its eyes never
meeting hers, never leaving her.

They pass two policía, this time they're dressed navy,

46

one policeman's eyes on the mongrel. He pulls his baton from the loop in his belt, pushes the dog with it, dog carries on after her. 'Perdón,' Policeman says, and shows her the underside of his hand.

He shoves the dog hard with his foot and it falls over, feet skitting across the brick with eyes rolling like oranges falling to the ground, or the roll of her father's fists when he was starting a fight, moustache a lump of charcoal crackling under his nose. 'It's Cuba, rotting his bones,' Mami used to say, but tapping her head. The dog stays on its side, gnashing its pale gums, drooping teats on its underside sunk into a cavern of ribs. Its outline dissolves in a moving network of fleas against sun-bleached brick of the pavement. Takes Cuba's focus away   brick brick   all the same, as she walks away.

As she moves, she feels her hips roll like her father's fighting fists, pumping her along until she reaches the port, stares at the yachts, tame sea.

As May turns to June to July she edges around the balconies of the hotel, room after room encircling the large swimming pool, her arms darken as the sun empties its hot lungs into the months.

She swipes the card to room 160, enters and her arm hairs rise up. A dark room confronts her, and then on turns a hanging bulb lit electric bright straight ahead of her, dust idles around it before falling in to kiss the glass. Beneath it, where the dresser should be, is a small round table standing on a straw mat, on it a bowl of oranges, agua de florida, a miniature bottle of rum, seven seashells and a statuette of the Virgin in blue.

'Mami?' she says. It isn't Mami, the room is too cold, the absence of love. She takes off her clothes, she has to, something hot running between her legs, kneels in front of the altar and closes her eyes. She holds out a hand, trying to conjure nothing into something, into the courage of a beating heart, feels an orange squeeze down her throat pushing her lungs apart gulps and swallows, and then starts to cry and out of her mouth comes birdsong, the parakeet, the nightjar, the whistling duck, the flycatcher, the vireo, the cartacuba, the bullfinch, breaking into a wail like a dog to a coarse howling baby's cry.

Light breaks into the room, soft through her eyelids, Noda has opened the curtains, bustles around, quick vowels barely pausing for breath. She breaks wind and laughs, a brief pause in her cursing and scolding.

'Sixteen more rooms you've got on this floor. Mierda! How are you this slow? Why am I helping you? You're lucky you look like someone I knew once. Fuck you.' She hastily pulls the sheets from the bed piling them onto the floor. 'Why do I find you so often   staring at the wall like that?'

Cuba goes to wipe the tears from her eyes, but they're dry.

Noda, crossing the room. 'This is too much for anyone, sore hands, broken knees, my blood pressure – it's stress. They'll notice you getting slow, are you sick?' she says, 'Ten cuidado. Take it easy, but work hard, Cuba.'

She mentions a meeting, why she came up to find her. Her voice disappears in a din of plastic bottles hollow-knocking from the bathroom.

She emerges, 'Are you coming?'

'Yes.' Without knowing to what.

'I'll send a message.' Noda leaves, fast as she came, her rubber shoes squeaking a loose sole.

The tiny courtyard of the bar smells of ash.

'There's a movement starting in Barcelona, we should do the same.' Noda is near shouting. 'Thirty rooms a shift, these sub-contractors are evil.' Her friend, who works in a hotel near the crypt, nods her head regular in time with music from the bar. A muted television screen high on the wall shows a forest on fire and a rising column of smoke, grey-yellow.

The day of the altar was a warning. Like Mami, the bad spirit had caught up with her, making itself known to her over and over, like the echoes of the objects in front of her eyes   spat out at regular points in space, a padlock, the moon, perpendicular to logic.

She sees the face of her baby in random encounters, a young boy in the street, a teenager she encountered in a corridor, young boys, baby boys encountered on the walk home   encountered   in the little boys running wet by the pool   skin a mass of drips of gold, in the faces she passes in the plaza in the cool hours, the child   encountered as the small brown bird shrieking at her from its perch in a tree, toenails lengthened to gripping claws. Child from the dark of her mind, intent on having her die of shame   ah   had her inflamed.

She feels the charm tight in a pocket, pulls at a coil in her hair and notices, from their table wedged in a corner, the manager from her first day, and another she's seen in the hotel, decorated with gold name badge, name beginning with 'E', he wears polished shoes long and square, upturned at the tips like rowing-boats. She taps Noda's arm and tells her the news, Noda freezes mid-sentence, turns and smiles them over, on the offensive. Manager, named Oko, has a little muscle pulsing beneath his eye, no smile but nods in her direction. 'E' introduces himself, speaks like his tongue is glued down,

she doesn't catch the name. She tries a smile her lips
sticky with vodka-lemonade. It gets busy. People edging
sideways past tables, holding cigarettes   smoke
tracing the path of the summer's rising heat. A heavy
feeling settles in her stomach. She forces out a cough.

There are more meetings like this. In bars, not so
much – in apartments, back rooms of churches, loaned
garages, the library, a word or two exchanged by lockers,
an arrangement, a touch of the hand: we need sick pay,
contracts, managers are nervous, the maids' faces give
nothing away.
    Noda comes by whenever their hours overlap, or
comes to her home. She runs by Cuba every tentative
word of an email, a bulletin, a speech for an audience
day by day becoming   less imaginary. Barcelona on
her lips, her mouth's oil, Lanzarote, Las Islas Canarias,
Ibiza, sticky over her fingers, combed through her hair.
Standing on her imagined podium, belly roll beneath her
shirt, her back straight, and calloused hand curled into a
fist. The same words are affirmed every time, sisterhood,
solidarity, love, freedom, truth   bleed into the daily
rhythm of the work: curtains pulled, sheets stretched flat
over mattress, spray, brush, cloth on glass, on glass, day
by day by day. Cuba's knuckles crack as she raises a pot
from the stove, pours coffee for the two of them. 'Work
and work and work, mija, until you're dead,' Mami used
to say, and laugh.
    And work, the work goes on, it does. Cuba edging
around the balconies feeling like she's being watched.
Oko edging around the balconies after her, ever nodding
in her direction, nothing better to do.

A Thursday, she dusts each crease of the heavy curtains, smooths down the bedding, scrubs the toilet, shower, wipes a towel over the bathroom marble until it shines enough, goes to leave room 188 and Oko stands in the doorway, holding a finger-width rail of wood which he waves around in a figure of eight in front of her face, looping around her head until his moderate skill loses its nerve. Showing off   a threat? Shall she be impressed? She makes a show of being impressed.

'Silambam,' he says at last, face and neck wearing a damp sheen, 'a martial art. Es de la India.' His shirt stretches tight across his belly as it throbs with quick breath, a glimpse of hair creeping close to the skin, black moss, curled like the dark hair on his head.

He continues to show up outside of the rooms she's working in. She has been keeping up the numbers, thirty rooms a shift, cutting corners, drinking up leftover wine, and swiping forgotten cigarettes, bottles of nail polish, alcohol, cologne and perfume. And he has never come with an accusation.

She's on the floor cleaning as he walks in, tapping the wall with that stick, then the floor, closer he moves. She's found a stain behind a dresser, no one has thought to look there, or had the time. Coffee, old stain has etched itself into the wall. She's been hypnotized by the rubbing, aching arms and shoulders but keeping it up, rubbing off the dark brown, releasing the wall's memories, the coffee – spilled or thrown – thin layers of paint, green, white beneath.

Oko taps her shoulder with the stick. Then, crouches to tap with a finger on her skirt at the crack of her ass. She doesn't turn around, yes her blood pressure is raised a little, and she has already decided that if he goes further she will submit. (Alone, rubbing her own breasts, swollen and ripe, legs opening to welcome her fingers between the tops of her thighs. What she thinks about at times like this, when what is about to happen happens.)

He stands up and leaves, because of her silence, perhaps. Or the charm always grasped in her pocket. Or a noise in the corridor outside. She doesn't see him on shift again. Whenever a group of them gather, he gives up his seat for her.

Another meeting, it's evening. Women and some children enter the room, sombre as a low-hanging mist. A mass of heads and clasped hands. They don't say much to each other, until Noda begins.

'We don't have the right to get sick
because   because
they fire us
immediately
health and skin
on the floors that we clean
god of fury
empower us.'

And people are on their feet, clapping hands together, fanning their faces with folded paper, or waving it above their heads. 'Fair pay, sisterhood, freedom,' chanted with the defiance of all the uprisings begun in a small room. The spirits, both good and bad, are present and alert. Cuba stands and cheers, soaking in the power of the hands beating as tight-skin drums. 'Sin muerto no hay santo,' 'There's no Orisha without the spirits of the dead,' the words in her ear, she's soon doubled over with a pain in her abdomen and a light head, having avoided water for the past few days, avoiding the toilet because she's pissing blood. She takes herself to the bathroom, quiet, but there are tiny flies fussing around the room, excited by the cheering, riding on reverberations in the air that will travel outwards indefinitely.

She sits in a cubicle and takes the charm from her pocket – digging into her – and asks for protection, for the bad spirit at her side to forgive. Ever since that day on the steps of the hospital, when she had put down the bag and started driving, there has been a dense mass in her mind, in her stomach, working its way through her. A seedless fruit lodged in her womb and rotting. Bad spirit   an imbalance that permeates all things, like the smoke from a bushfire thousands of miles away, where sky glows the amber of flame, breaking in new days, new afternoons.

The toilet door opens. 'Cuba,' Noda says. The movements of her arm in flickering light as she bats away the flies.

'Sí, Noda.' From the cubicle. Gripping her belly.

'Estás bien?'

'Estoy enferma. Don't worry, go back in there.' A quick in-breath.

'Have you done a test?'

'No it's not that. Not that.'

'Oh honey, qué mierda.' Noda's hand appears in the gap beneath the door, flexing and wriggling her fingers in some kind of solidarity. Her face appears skin drooping to one side. She's a grown woman, Noda, Cuba finds the space to think of that. Slow tears reach her chin and drip into her hands.

Baby's cry had pealed out through the bag when she reached ten metres away. Her aching arm remembers the baby boy's soft weight, her ears, the cry that clung to her as she resisted any urge to look back.

'Cuba, don't worry,' Noda's disembodied head says from the floor. 'We'll take care of it. Sometimes bad things infect us. We'll sort it out, I'm telling you. Come on, Cuba. It's just one bad thing   that's all it is.'

HEARTBREAK AT THE SUPER 8

Ursula loves me
she loves
the way sunlight
                    touches
the exposed parts of me
                    and my insides are warmed
                                        by its touch
sometimes   it burns

her love will burn a hole through me

Early June, she found me, laid out ten yards from my
motorcycle, consumed by dust and grit which grated the
flesh beneath my fingernails, my hands, forearms, side
of my face. Skin was parched, lips cracked deep, dry and
raw as desert grooves. She gave me a drink, asked me
what happened. I gave her nothing but face blank as my
mind, she helped me into her truck anyhow.

She drove with me in the front seat, the wind knocked
out of me. With one arm she pulled a blanket over my
body.

'My friend,' she said, 'she made it.'

The blanket reminded me of SpaghettiOs – red
gingham, same colour as the label on the can.

'Spaghetti,' I said.

'You need a doctor?' she asked.

'Nah.' I rubbed my eyes.

I watched the road, trying to get my bearings. The sky
was clear and up ahead yawned a mountain pass. The
mountains were retreating, trying to shrug us off. Arm
outstretched, I ran a finger over their outlines.

'You still feeling funny?' she said.

'Trying to figure it out.'

'You got special powers in them fingertips?'

'We're on the I-80, I know that much.' Road signs rushed by.

'Coming up to Fernley, two miles,' she said.

'That's nearly all the way.'

'I figured you were headed this way, from where I found you.'

She looked over at me, taking her focus off the road, her eyes were a mournful grey, with shallow crow's feet fanning out from the corners, cut by blonde.

Shrubs and cactuses shot past the windows.

'You remember what happened?'

'No.' I remembered riding, I remembered her face over mine, but nothing useful. 'Is the bike beat-up?'

'Some scratches, you couldn't have been going fast. It's in the back.'

'Thanks,' I said.

'You don't have anything on you,' she said, 'you should call the police.'

'It's okay, I haven't been robbed,' I said, feeling my wallet tucked into my boot.

'So you fell from heaven?' she laughed, coughed, rolled down the window and air tore into our compartment like we were crashing in from outer space, watching the earth come into view.

'So what are you doing in Reno?' Collar flapping around her neck.

'Work.' A half-truth. 'You?'

She gave a faint smile.

'What kinda work you doing?' I said.

'Hotel work.'

'Hotel work?'

'Yeah, it's a fancy hotel.'

She didn't ask where I was from or my name even. I didn't ask her either. She only asked how I was feeling. I offered to pay her for the trouble, she declined. I asked her to let me out after Fernley. 'Can do,' she said, then went on to her hotel.

I checked into the Super 8, stretched out on the bed and slept, showered, coughing like my lungs were full of sand, went to find something to drink. I sat at the counter, hunched over, nose to my beer like a bloodhound.

I imagined Blondie's fancy hotel. Red velvet interiors above a casino, like the Grand Sierra, with her at the front desk, eyelids powder pink and that floating colour, rouge, on her cheeks, checking guests into the spa or the restaurant: gold Rolex watches, big moustaches, chain-link necklaces, white teeth, clean fingernails – the Devil's welcome if he can afford it.

My thoughts were cut off by a belch, the guy sitting two down from me was shovelling triple eggs and fried potatoes into his mouth, with a beer same as mine.

He caught me looking.

'Can I help you?' he said. A brush of moustache curled around his mouth, reminded me of my father, grey with lines of skunk black and white, his lip a pink wet clam peeking out the bottom, the quiet concentration on his face as he holds my hand under a stream of scalding water. His car scratched by my bicycle. My bicycle dented. I must learn to pray for my boyish soul, boy needs a lesson teachin and my daddy has backwards ways and backwards words.

'Son?'

'Sorry.' I put my nose back to my beer.

I felt the air move and heard the chink of a plate on

the counter to my left. He was real close.

'Carson.' He held out his hand.

'Hi.'

'No name?'

'J.'

'Welcome.'

Red-faced, a trucker, and no stranger to the place, he told me. He loosened his pants as he ate, the stool whined a little as he leaned forward, rubbing his bacon in maple syrup like those winter athletes I'd seen on TV, curling.

In spite of all the eating, he talked, mouth grinding like a waste disposal.

'Where you headed?'

'Reno.'

'Why'd you stop here for?' He laughed. 'That's like taking your foot off the gas just before the top of the hill.'

'I got nowhere to stay in town. I'll ride in tomorrow.'

A red-haired waitress came and slipped some bacon onto his plate. He put his arm around her thick waist, the bottom of her dress was tight over her thighs and her hips peaked like the hills, far away outside.

'Jenny, you're something else,' he said.

'How many years you been coming here and you ain't learned my name?'

'I know your name, Jeanie.' He picked up a strip of bacon and folded it into his mouth. 'I just like Jenny better. It's my dog's name.'

She slapped him lightly on the shoulder, then looked at me. 'You eating?'

'Not just yet,' I said. She went back to work.

'You divorced?' he said.

I didn't answer.

'Separated, me,' he said, and laughed again. I couldn't

60

figure out why, but the laughing made me want to talk.

'I'm here to get some things.' My gun, my hat, my shoes. 'Wanna make some money,' I said, 'she still lives in Reno.'

'And now you live?'

'With friends out-of-state, different places.'

'I hear ya,' he said, 'we're all just passing through heartbreak here.' His voice racked up a gear and he yelled, 'Heartbreak at the Super 8!'

He laughed again, I laughed, he raised his beer, so did I, as did a few other guys standing over at the pool table. We drank and kept drinking till our eyes felt wet and loose. He told me about a fight he'd had with his brother, who was on crutches. He grabbed the thing from under his arm and let him fall into a ditch. I wasn't so good at telling stories, mainly we talked about getting into fights, and women. We willed the night to roll on forever, gave into that sinking feeling as we turned the corner into morning.

I went to the restroom, Carson came in after me. Hung his arm over my shoulders while I peed.

'Tell you what,' he said, his breath carried the stench of the night. 'You take your broken heart down to the Wild Horse ranch.'

'What's that?'

'What's that!' he said, and his neck reeled in. 'Why'd she ever get ridda you?'

He put his hand on my dick. I pushed him away and did up my pants. He raised his hands.

'Okay honey,' he said, and took himself to the urinal. He turned around again to face me, spilling pee on his shoes. 'For when you're lonely, divorcee. Wild Horse Canyon Drive.'

I rode towards the city, the sun high, eyes still blinkered from the night. Then I saw the turning. My gut sent me to the right, down an empty road until I saw the ranch up ahead. There was a parking lot out front stretched wide as the sea.

I walked through a doorway guarded by girls with neon breasts. They flashed on off, as if to tease my appetite. The inside no different, ornate and cheap, smelled like patchouli and baby oil. Someone greeted me and sat me down, a glass of water for my cough, told me to wait for the girls. I was facing some purple drapes, hiding things I wasn't supposed to see.

They walked in one by one. Women's bodies in a moving line, perfectly painted pink, red and orange mouths smiled hi

my name's Sylvie, Jenny, Clara,
she after she
with the red hair
she with the scarred eye
she with her heart open
she who had been shot in the head
she the blonde
hi, I'm Ursula
she who found me fallen by the roadside

Ursula? Blondie, dressed up all fancy, shorts, yellow tube top, high heels.

'So this is your hotel?' I said as we walked down the hall.

'This is it.' She looked pleased to see me, lips curled to a smile as she opened the door to her room.

It wasn't what I'd expected, seemed more like a person lived there. That gingham blanket was folded in the corner. On the wall was a poster of a skinny guy in pantyhose holding a ballerina. She was a foot from the ground, a surprised look – eyebrows arched, head cocked to the side like a broken fence post.

'Nice poster,' I said.

'The Nutcracker,' she said. 'Do you know it? It's beautiful.' As if to tell me there was a life far from here she could be living. I looked at her.

'Alright, angel?' she said.

I said yeah. Then the sun came through the window shade and hit her chest. Yellow travelled up her neck, face. She was the most beautiful thing I'd seen. There was a cave in me, some emptiness that was always there. I felt it grow deeper, louder, close to unbearable and then in one screaming moment, it was filled, and said to me my name.

    she puts a hand on my neck
                warm as the sun

    then she says   so honey, what'll it be?

I headed into Reno to get my things. My ex had kept them all these months, but cursed me as I stood at the front door. Why did I ride all that way to be standing there? They're just two sides of the same coin, love and hate, I realized as I flipped her goodbye for the last time. All my possessions I wore – my gun, my hat and leather shoes. The boots I'd been wearing I threw away.

I spent what was left of the day, night and next morning downtown. I was mesmerized by the lights of the cosmos that hit me as I rode down Virginia Street, got high on those delirious avenues, lights so bright they'll strip you bare, shooting stars flew through my

side mirrors, made me feel lucky. I thought of Blondie in
her little room.

    she was glad I came
               my body is warmed
               by her touch

    I made myself a hundred dollars at a half-moon table,
lost most of it on the slot machines, won fifty, had some
drinks and something to eat.

    I was looking for work fixing machines in casinos.
All the strange and lost people of the world find shelter
in these places. Drink in my hand I watched a woman
eat her way through a bag of cherries. They went into
her mouth fat and shiny, her lips sucking in like a snail
frightened into its shell, she spat out the pits behind her.
Nobody said a thing so long as she played. When people
walked past you could hear the pits pop under feet, but
they all looked up for the noise. You don't know down
or up inside those places, day or night, yes or no. My
guy said come back tomorrow, so I bought some gas and
headed back to the Wild Horse.

She was surprised I didn't ask for anything special: no
extra mirrors, massage, deep throat, anal, just straight
fucking.

    I stood by the door to her room for a short time,
waiting for the sun to hit her body again, but today it was
in the wrong place. No mind.

    I put my hand in her hair, tied up, parted to let my
fingers through. I could smell it, something strawberry.
She took out the hair tie. At the roots her blonde was
swallowed into dark   dark brown. I combed her hair
to the side with my fingers to see more of it. Think I was

too rough as she took my hand away and put it lower down, on her breast.

And then what? The bottom of her top, my thumbs and forefingers I use to lift it as she raises her arms I pull it up, off.

A drip of sweat from my hairline runs down the wrinkle in my forehead to my nose. Don't want to wipe it, for her to see it. Two more come to join it. Her eyes on mine the whole time. I forget about it. I'm getting hard, swelling into my jeans.

She unzips me, we undress. She goes to the bed and sits with her back to the wall, knees up, then lets her legs fall to part, and I ache. I ache for her when she's right there, she's retreating, sinking into the wall. I go over to her don't feel my feet moving. I'm just there with her looking up at me. She lets me put a finger in her mouth, won't let me kiss her but I get close enough to take in the smells of her body, sweet as fruit and sweat: the dry ends of her hair, her feet, her mouth. A body-halo thick as heat stuck in the air. I run my finger, still wet, over her collarbone, over the skin-fold at her hip, down to the smooth skin between her thighs.

She grabs my hand and pulls me towards her, 'Relax.' I lie on my back, condom, her hand working it on, gripping me her nails long in lavender, before she climbs on top of me, moving her hips back and forth. She sighs and the window shade beats on its hinges, her hot breath is the wind and it blows through me.

I put a hand to her throat, 'Say J.' She says it, the name vibrates under my fingers. Lift my hips and let go   in me, grab the soft edges of her legs and for a couple seconds my body crying of thirst is quenched. She

red-lipped

with angel wings fucks me to heaven

whence I fell

I grab a breast, hips   it's not enough
my lungs can't be filled enough
I'm not filled enough
this is gonna kill me

my mouth open moan
or an amen

I told her that she was all I wanted and would ever
need. Her red lipstick, her face and her laugh.

She told me it was business business business, but I
knew that she was holding something back. With her
hands and lips she wasn't holding back. Her eyes on
mine and me inside of her. I had seen her dark roots,
dark as those hidden curls between her thighs.

I decided, as I rode through the hot air of that day, to
stick around a while longer. Back to the Super 8. I was
sure I could see the back of the ranch from a distance,
through a gap in the rocky hills, sprawling, flat and
brown. There was the swimming pool, the sandstone
patio yellow against the blue above. Myself lost under
blue, hawks circling fixed my eyes, stopped my mind
from spinning.

I went into town to work. Waiting for the money to
come in was like being made to count every full stop in
the Bible. When the money did come it was in crisp rolls
of cash that smelled like drywall. I gambled some of it
and sometimes got lucky, counting it in, counting it out,
but with her every dollar was multiplied, jackpot every
time, with a rain of golden paper strips and as I catch

them on my tongue, taste of gold is surprising – limes, watermelon, sometimes buttered pancakes or egg yolk. I counted on multiplying my dollars with Ursula, she who never spit nails out at me. I went to her, she was always there. The heat of the afternoon was less of a beating, more like an embrace.

One day, I saw her downtown. I watched as she parked her truck and walked fast in sneakers down the crowded boulevard, then turned into a quieter street. The glint of the afternoon curved over parked cars, speeding into flashes as I moved faster to keep behind her, like the flash of lemon-white and the knife that slices. The Reno-white flashes of tan and teeth. She turned and looked straight at me. Didn't realize I was crouched low until I heard the sound of water dripping, and the smell, a dog pissing on a hubcap by my knee. I stayed there until she went into a salon, some guy's arms embraced her shoulders. I waited for her to come out again, but when she did my body started heaving, coughing. Next time I looked up, she was gone.

Alone in my room I lay face up on my bed, listening to my lungs rattle, flies circled the ceiling fan in tune with the hawks outside. I thought about Blondie, us making love. I tried to find pictures of her online, decorate the place a little, but was out of luck. I could reconstruct her in my mind from the toenails up and get her right. I was never one for drawing, but I did try, and kept the picture on my nightstand it was something. Nights, she would step outside of my memory and into my room at the Super 8, breath in my ear. I would find strands of blonde hair on the pillow next to me.

With no extra cash to visit, I'd go to the Wild Horse saloon for a drink just to see her and talk. It was open on weekends and some nights. The cave in my chest

housed a monster in flame, my insides licked by fire
and eaten away as the minutes passed. But when the
women entered the saloon she always stood still for a
moment, eyes hovering over the room like a hawk on the
wing, looking for me. I played the game, always sat in a
different place.

> bless this woman
>
> who looks for me across the room
> and comes to me
> her feet untainted by the ground

This time, her roots were blonde. Her hand touched
mine, warm wanting love. I asked her why she dyed her
hair, I liked it before. And who dyed it? Was it a man?
Was he a friend?

'You just keep to your own,' she said, and pinched my
nose with her knuckles.

With no money even for the saloon, I'd wait around
downtown. She wouldn't be at the hair salon again for a
while. So I waited by the bank some days, grocery stores
or nail salons. Other days, I would sit on the bed and
look out towards the hills, or stay out in the yard and
aim my gun at the zebra-tails, those lizards didn't even
run, just froze when they felt my shadow, didn't even
know what a gun was or how I could blow them away if
I wanted.

I made love to Ursula, and after, she was acting weird,
sad, distracted. I had one of the pictures I'd drawn folded
in my pocket, wanted her to have it. Thought it was
raining outside but no, her nails drumming the wall.

'You alright?' I said.

'Yeah, course, until next time honey.' Avoiding my

eyes. She had scratches on her arms.

I stopped what I was doing, walked over. 'What's this?' I said reaching out, she took a step back.

'I fell, by the pool there,' and pointed to the window shade, closed. 'Should be more careful huh?'

'So you fell too, from heaven,' I said.

She smiled, but then she said, 'Yeah, straight into hell.' I had a dark feeling about it. 'You're all healed up?' She was looking at my forearms, faint pink scars from the day we met. 'Amazing isn't it? We all heal up like that,' she moved further away, looking in the mirror, tying her hair in a knot. 'I think that when you heal, the skin grows stronger, thicker. You won't get hurt the same way again...' she trailed off, rubbed her arms. 'Speaking of hell, the heat here at the moment, I need a break from it. I'll be off in a day or so.'

'How long?' I said, something big as an orange choking my throat.

'Oh a couple weeks, nothing much.'

'Where?'

'To see a cousin.'

'You'll come back?' I said.

'Sure will.'

I had her word. I've said my own vows and broken them. I left that room uneasy, with a flat mind.

The cough worsened. I coughed sand onto the bed as I slept. I would wake up with it grinding in my ears after dreaming of being swallowed by quicksand, last thing I'd see was my hand outstretched against the blue. I would try to cough it all up, retching until sweat leaked to the floor.

It was as if my meeting her had put me on a new course. Intervention. Then, the thought came to me clean as a shooting star.

She'll come with me, heading north to Idaho or
Montana, where the air's cooler. I'll find work in the
outdoors. She won't have to work any more. I could buy
land, build a house or buy a small one if I save enough. I
would do my best, my best to keep her.

Ursula
I will take us into the cool air

we shall cough the dust from our lungs and
breathe clean again

I went back the next day to tell her the plan. Saw her
truck parked outside.

I sat alone, facing those purple drapes. Did they have
people hiding back there? Watching. I went over to
look behind them, it was so dark everything went black
until my eyes could pick out the things piled there:
shoes, women's shoes, must've been about fifty pairs in
different colours, and a door sunk deep into the wall.
A noise, the girls were coming out. They looked at me
smiling hi but Ursula wasn't there. My insides dropped.
I said sorry, and left. As I rode away the wind beat on me
in dry heaves and nearly threw me off.

I reached the end of the driveway and waited off-road,
watched every car and truck pass by. I was there until
the last men drove out, some girls went by too but those
whores were good for nothing but dust, they were rats in
the sand.

When the saloon opened its doors hours later I went
and bought a whiskey, was told to kindly wait. The place
took thirty minutes to fill up with men eager to talk to
women.

Ursula came out – they all came out – through a red

door. Heads turned and it went quiet for a second, before a bunch of whooping and cheering. I was impatient. She was in blue. As she sat by me I told her in a rush everything I'd been thinking over. I said that I was serious and she wasn't to laugh it off.

'There's other clients I gotta see,' she said.

'I'm not a client,' I told her.

She brushed her nail over my cheek while turning away, toward eager eyes. But I took her pinky and wouldn't let go. I held on tight, squeezing through the sweat of my hand. It was all I could do to fight the storm whipping up inside of me. I pulled her back to me and felt her finger bones crack

one

two

three   and her eyes on me, wide on me, white and round. I didn't mean to cause hurt. I was surrounded by a wall of men, they put me out of there too fast for me to do anything, couldn't say sorry. No cops, but they didn't want me back.

I paced my room at the Super 8 like an animal, opened every drawer, the closet, the cabinet, as if the answer lay in there. My neck, my face, my balls burned, heat spread up my spine. I bent over to breathe better, coughed till my gut ached. Then I touched on the picture in my pocket, I'd forgotten.

I loaded my gun, outside I felt the heat rolling in with the sound of the grasshoppers, the hawks. Took a shot at a zebra-tail and blew it straight through its middle. Its eyes were open and tail moving like it was running, along with the back legs, toes splayed out with tiny claws and the meat of it spread across the ground – pink watermelon, juice swallowed up by the earth, no mess. I fired again, into the air. I could hear shouting behind me, didn't turn around. Footsteps rushing, up and down stairs, away from me.

She's afraid of me.

I squinted my eyes in the direction of the Wild Horse. I couldn't see it. Just the dark outlines of the hills, and then I felt my knees hit the ground, started to pray, started to cry.

> house of angels   take us to heaven
> as she with the neon breasts
> watches over us from   the outside
> we   thin and fragile
> suffer quietly
> this long road
> is too hard to travel
>   we are the link between heaven
> and earth
> acknowledge the truth of our lives
>   Amen

I just want to take us there. My gun   my hand doesn't know what to do, it's weak as my mind is. A noise, like someone pounding wood with their fist. A woman screeching. I hear a door shutting and then footsteps, dampened by earth, rushing towards me.

> her hot breath is the wind
> in the heat of today she glows yellow in sunlight
> and sun falls from her hair in violet rays
> and nothing compares
> to her touch
>   oh   baby
>
>   it's the best

THE GROWING STATE

The Winner crushes white pills crackle pop under
the bank card heavy. So heavy is the bank card black,
money, wow, so rich, so fly, so   dry is the grainy
powder crushed pills cracking under the flat card that
is platinum heavy. Hoovers up, teeth bared, and the
curled lips of 'H'. Swallows the stinging drip. Again
nose to powder, bank note snorting chokes it back
because the powder   is dry. Eyes roll up with the
sunrise burning through the window glass, the room
dissolves, the phone rings. Yes? And he stretches out a
steady hand to unhook it but no steady hand appears.
I'm looking at you, to the arm lying limp on the desk,
the arm is somewhere in his past and failed to keep
up – as punishment – goes to chew the arm, growls at
the shirt sleeve, so he thinks, bites at his own shoulder,
so he might believe, the intention not lived out, the
jaw is slack and so remains, looking to that arm again
to move a steady hand towards the ringing phone but
no steady hand appears, cheek to carpet body releases
dust in heavy landing, now lying on his right side, the
phone rings out as he retches heavy liquid, warm down
the cheek, nose a flow to the ocean, crisp burning eyes
and bile smell, nipples cold, chest squeezed under his
own great weight. Doctor, prognosis, is this me done?
The prized shark one thousand kilo'd cut loose for his
brothers and sisters hungry at sea, amen.
    Quiet.
    Winner? I am he on the floor. Judders his bones
laughing. Welcomes the ghosts to come and drink, to
crack open a bottle from his cabinet. Antiquated glass.
Brown and old wood smell of humidity and humours,
breathing over this white and new – smooth interiors,

curved chairs, floor to ceiling glass, slanted logo letter
writing, the floor in white to reflect it. A heavy wood
desk and cabinet stubbornly remain. Ghosts and the
living to come and drink, the ones he barely remembers,
he has ignored.

I   am he. Cut me loose, amen.

How long am I here, in tight trousers and panting?
And lost at sea? No, saliva pouring from my mouth
a surf lapping at my cheek. Flat out, hot feeling. Yes,
this office room brighter than ever, powder falling from
the walls, is all that I've absorbed into myself spat out?
Mercy. All the smokes are smoked. God   is on the
edge of a knife, the cutting blade. So off with my hair.
Off with the shirt and tie and trousers. Let me be naked,
thank you. And quickly, go.

The phone, again.

Someone speaks through the machine. Ottessa runs
through the week: 'You don't want to be disturbed, I
know, but a reminder.' She's standing up, voice full and
assertive. 'Morning meeting tomorrow, 9 a.m., over at
Tullow's offices, good luck, I've emailed you the briefing
notes, car booked for 8.40 car back to the office, let me
know, car home car booked afternoon lunch pre-ordered
then we have them coming in, I know, there was no other
day table across the road booked for dinner, breakfast,
I thought that you would be hungry, let me know, safe
trip, your flight for Wednesday booked for 9 p.m. as
you asked need your sign-off on those expenses at
some point and those and those, lunch meeting with the
lawyers when you're back please let me know, I know,
please let me know, and Sam will go with you, it looks
better for us, in his words, in our words, good luck, safe
trip, next time.'

Next time. Thirst is laughter, with laughter quenched

and emptied again. That's the joke. With my hands I try drag this lump of body over the white, towards the door ahead. The pot plant bristles. These fingers couldn't move the fat, the blubber of this man one inch, couldn't drag him away from this hole already dug out. Desperate fingers wail, moving like the legs of a beetle, each one crimping, curling, relaxing, until stiffening all at once.

'He's that way again.'

That cleaner never knocks. Appears at the door in tiny size, like a figurine of porcelain, hello, then grows larger and larger to my eyes until dusting everything off around me. She's the one to find me then, she's the one to swallow this yeasted stench of my spread like proving dough. She'll be the one to push me into silence, my glutinous form, eroding bones, loosening hinges and lolling neck, into the earth to deflate, decay.

'Sir, I always knock. Try to be calm.'

You knocked? Little figurine in the corner, statuette. I heard no knock. As you're afraid of cracking, no doubt. Those figurines should be made illegal, out-of-law, stop my mother-in-law packing my home with little clowns, dogs, girls with umbrellas all gathering dust. I suppose you'd know about dust, woman?

'I know more than I'd care to know. And what state are you in today? I usually find you sleeping upright, or beneath the desk, worked a night, or carried on the party alone, or with some girl maybe. I don't know. Always something. You, in the middle of this office, and I'm to work *around* you, as usual, and the grand sad desk thrusting out of this white and new, working around your blunt sensibility, hoovering up your poor choices, cleaning powder from the desk. The smell of thirst hovers above your body, so long since you drank.'

My own thirst? I bleat like a body without a head, an open throat. What is the smell of thirst, woman? Like eggs, lavender, or watermelon? No, dry grass, wouldn't you say? Or hot charcoal, pig skin burning hairs, and sugar caramelizing, hardening itself in the corners of my eyes, woman clean them, I can't close them now.

'I'll get to it. But first the room, it won't wait. These half-empty shelves, the little containers, are the pills to help you sleep? Some exotic names, Efexor, the depressive type? Two books and this cabinet full of drink, and oranges to eat at least. All covered in powdered grey   you just breathe out dust, don't you? Look how he stares, straining his eyes he looks around, a small circumference.'

Yes woman, he stares at a cigar stub and a folded piece of paper beneath the cabinet. Paper covered in words, for what? The cigar-remnant of a celebration, but when? The words, can I remember writing? The mind a deep well, remembering, winding the wheel. I pull a bucket up from its depths and find it full of dark water, or bones, or fish, or oil and strain to see deeper into the knowing, from not knowing. Feeling nothing down my right side. On hitting the floor there was the scrape of rough sleeve, friction was a thousand tiny fingernails drawing across my body, heat on the back of my hand. Now there's the faint trace of an arm drawn in pencil line, nothing felt, shaded or filled in. And the note of paper? There were days when I wrote notes to a wife, to friends. Until recently I still had thoughts to express. Until recently – a lie – until years ago.

The room heating up, all this glass. Better to have a house of mud, where coolness rules, and coolness sounds like running water's echo. The sound of heat? Crickets chirping. Long grass snapping in the wind, dry crackling from my throat as air escapes, so long since I drank. And now, as I deflate, I feel the cavern within, an emptiness ready to collapse into the ground, taking all the room with me.

'The phone. Shall I answer?'

Yes, woman.

'You might not like what they have to say, is why I ask. I call myself Lucida, and you can call me that now.'

Get me the phone and hold it to my upwards ear. So many calls unanswered already, I can't miss this.

'Too late.'

On and off flashing light a message.

My wife's voice,   'I'm afraid to ask the question. Just washed my hair   shampoo ran into my left eye, a dry sting my eye scrubbed clean. It's only slightly redder than the other from a bad night's sleep. And a leak, from beneath the bathroom sink, blood from my gums as I flossed my teeth ran out onto the floor with water   leaked. The question, can I look at myself in the mirror and say, through bleeding gums, that I, your third nameless wife, have a place in our home, leave a groove in the bed when I get up in the night? I do love you. You seem surprised when I say it. Your eyebrows raise – or wince? I'm afraid to ask, do we have a life together? With no children I   you're a man I'm with, feeling our way in the dark towards the end. I'm afraid I have questions: do you sleep when you are away at night? When the house is emptied of you. Who with? Are we lost to each other? I'm afraid I   oh. I'm hungry, and I taste blood. Ah well.'

'Your wife wants your attention.'

She has lost the plot. Lost, never lost, I am never. At night I put myself in a place I choose. She is cold. If I'm away it's because of that. Ices me out, I slip. I *seem* absent because her cold-exuding body can't feel the warm, or a living thing close by, bitch   is cold. I love you she says. I wince. Now it rains.

'Weather changes from this to that in a second. And now, getting on to wiping those eyes and vomit from beneath your face. Cleaning spit from your cheeks, sweat from the grooves in your neck. And this blood? A trail, jagged path across your shirt. What did you do?'

A bite. I think. It was never supposed to get so rough.

'You bite? I don't believe it. Ah, a wedding ring, cutting, your hands are bloated, your feet. I'll take off your shoes to relieve them some, the ring, I'm afraid, will have to stay.'

The ring can stay, a binding document after all – says much about it – in the end it cuts so deep and eventually slices off a finger. And out of the bloodied stump there grows   not a new finger, but a leaf bud.

'Not what you'd expect, granted. But green life does tend to grow when it's raining. And as the rain is sloshing the windows, sky darkened, I'll turn on the light so you can look around. I've seen all this before, every inch of this room you've forsaken.'

That's because the inches of this room are dull, and drink is better. But the desk and the cabinet I like and insist on keeping. Hold back the persistent creep of the white and new, shiny and bold, slanted logo letter writing, that Ceropegia for my 'wellbeing'. That powder floats above the floor as a mist, dissipates, dampening everything, all is tinged with green and softening with growing moss.

'The room softens for you yes, and the room loves you, yes.'

Love. If only I could spell the word. Imagine the air stratified into its component parts: a strip of hydrogen, helium, methane, neon, nitrogen, oxygen, argon, carbon dioxide, and the inconsequentials, krypton and xenon. Imagine a life surviving between the strata, that's me, balancing my intake of each – oxygen, yes, but not too much, to get light-headed and fall to xenon, say, then I'd be done for. Keep at the right level, too low and perish, too high, and perish. Love? Love is the hardest thing. To use up all your oxygen and die! Life is any kind of survival. Crouch, but don't get on your knees, and live, head forever bouncing between the nuclei.

'I can't say that makes much sense to me. You're overthinking it. I can see that you like explaining how it is, you tell me how it is, Winner, when I can see   it is. It is.'

The phone again, cries of thirst. Now I have eyes for the things around me, see the phone ringing violently, urgently, almost shakes enough to travel small small towards the edge of the desk, held in place by the cord plug.

Breast collapses in,
breath wheezes out,
a cloud of dust, it lands
and sound of water drip.

Lucida, why won't you answer it? Though I doubt I could form the words to speak.

'Winner, it's Number Two.' I called her the Number Two wife – I like to be smart with names. She never argued. 'Because I'm more than that to you, I know, sticks and stones.' A deep breath, 'Winner, ours was an abrupt end.' The machine catches her tongue, every sigh, lip licked and smacked to lubricate her next words transmutes into digital fuzz. 'We had everything to play for, and we did, and we had beautiful children, you were the biggest joy, the biggest disappointment.'

Kids grown and far flung, South Africa, Australia.
Practically chased them there myself, they're
embarrassed by me, the work I did, I do, and poisoned by
their mother – what can I say, weak minds. I should've
spent more time, more. They're far away. Good. Raise
their happy children. In the beginning I never much
wanted children, but now the urge, like to vomit, to see
them. To see my own blood fresh and living.

'Beautiful children, but we weren't a family. A body
without a head, Winner, we couldn't make a f—'

She goes on, voice singing in low tones I can't stand.
I provided, yes, as much as I could. Shall I repeat it?
About the air, the oxygen, the argon? That's enough.
Everything that woman uttered was a contradiction.
Winner be at home more they miss you. Child-rearing
is work too. But we had a nanny Number Two, a tutor,
a cleaner, we had it, I provided! Be home more, you're
missing everything about them. They need better
schools. You can't be away too long, too much. Away
getting her nails done, her lips. Away, what does it
mean? Even when I was there, I was accused of being
away. I'm done. She's done. Turn her off.

'She's gone, okay. Number Two has gone. Our mouths
are full of contradictions, Winner, our bad breath, the
reek of sullen hearts in our throats.'

Yes, bad breath of contradictions. I have loved,
not everything is sour, I have been loved. My head is
thumping the thrum thrum of an old conveyor belt
turning. A gun in my eyeline. Suitcase being searched
through. Did you pack your own bags Madam, where
are you travelling from, and you're staying with? With?
Are you telling us the truth, Madam? Your child, but
your child is...? Adopted. Right. And the bag, the little
one? Your child's bag yes, please give it. Mother kneels

to my level, smiles a smile cracked, mouth quivering. I am   crying? Her mouth says never mind to my cheek and the heat from her breath spreads and evaporates, leaving it cold.

Your memory or mine, Lucida? That memory so far away, washed to the bone. Composed of some unliveable real.

'Have it as yours. I have so many just like it anyway. I'll undo your tie now it's pretty tight, your jacket will come off next. Hold on.'

Time is slowing to a stop. In its death throes fragments of life, once dormant, stashed on the shelves of this room where I spent all my hours, come to me. Still moments of time stashed away in the half-empty room, and you, Lucida, speak my words.

Someone knocks light on the door, then sharp and heavy. Places ear to door and pause. The sound of dampened footfall strike of a heel away, then fainter, then nothing.

I am here   I wonder, in what sense. To them, office people, I am the boss. Their boss now a barnacle stuck to the floor, with tidy ears forced to listen to their knocks and footsteps. Are they afraid of me? I never wanted fear running across the office floor. The boil of hell on your knuckles knocking to speak to the boss. And what they say to my face. You're still young. You've kept smart, Winner. I don't know how you do it. Your edge, your devil may care, your stories hahaaa, they laugh at my jokes and say I'll buy you a drink. They say thank you, mentor. They say yesterday's a dirty word for people like us, Winner. Jutting elbows into my ribs. I lap it up, Winner is the light around which they orbit, the source of every tomorrow so long as they live. And where are they   now?

Yesterday is a dirty word in this business, more
and more there are troubles forcing me to look back.
I've been good at amassing fortunes. Finding and
monetizing. Bury it here or in Gibraltar. Panama. And
I was caught yes, once or twice or three. Avoiding tax
and other payments, here and there, workers' pensions
gone awry. The public are angry. Sure yes. But I tell you,
it's so hard to think of the workers when they're abroad,
or in some part of the city you never go. Yes. Enjoyed
what I was doing much, too much to rectify it, too much
thinking of the tomorrows, thinking of this business
business business. And now they come after us. My
today is 'public relations' meet with Mr. and Ms. X and
Y and appear compliant, but I want tomorrow, I want it
back.

Where is she? Somewhere behind my back and
knowing I can't turn around. Light hangs above my
head,
a draught   it swings a little,
shadow passes over the wall
revealing, crack in the paint.
A siren runs past, through my mind.
I am the siren now, a wave flung into the air.
Even a man like me knows the pleasure of seeing
a thick line of trees tearing across his eyeline, against
backdrop of blue, or a harsh rain tears to my eyes. Even
fat-headed man like me can watch a cat from his window,
slowly closing its eyes to the sun. Hear the tall grass
snap. Cup the scene like the hands cup a bowl, now the
bowl is empty. Only the mind's eye – the black pearl,
into the cat's eye, calm and obvious to itself. In many
things I failed, but they're humanity's faults, not mine
alone. And they come after me, that's the joke.

The clinch of gravity pulls on my joints. Mashes

my face.

'Yes, gravity pulls. Slows us down, brings us to a halt. Old fragments of time catch up with us. Never in the right order, mind you, never in the way that you thought you were.'

You're still here, cleaning my sick?

'No, all done with that. You hadn't noticed your jacket and shirt removed, your belt and socks? Don't feel any lighter? Or even the grass pushing up beneath you?'

The room overturned to grass, I can feel it now. And moss lining my windpipe and lungs, exhalations damp and heavy. That plant is overgrowing, a slow monster can't fight it back, thick leaves hanging over my head, dipping into my ears and eyes, covering the window, the shelves. The rain has cleared, and over half the day passed. So quickly. That phone light flashes again. What will the next one say? I don't want to hear.

'Father, Dad, she has two teeth now, I wanted to tell you that. You were always fond of numbers, counting: counting out the boats on the horizon, counting the steps down to the pool, counting the bats swooping over our heads, counting dead moths on the windowsill. Those are a few things I remember. I'm far away. I'm like a stranger, you were fond of me though, I know. Here she is (a gurgle) we'll count the teeth in and then count them out, falling, one, two, three, eh Winner? We'll come to visit you next time we're over, come to count the hairs on your chin. What else is there to do? Soon I'll be counting out my own teeth, if I'm lucky, counting the hairs in my ears already, counting the brown spots on the back of your hand, Winner? Count us in, Dad, count us out. You have a baby, then you see death emerging from the dark inside of your mouth. It was in you all along. I didn't see that coming, no no. There's so much more to say, words are gone.'

Bats swooping over our heads, I see them. Can't strain my neck to count. The boy had quicker eyes I much resented. His freedom of mind I resent. To punish a child for being better than you could have been, the kind of father I was. Couldn't swallow the compulsion to do harm. Can't reel back the damage, no hope of that. He was bright, moved away. A son. A granddaughter. Urge to see my own blood living, fresh and red, flushing a baby's cheeks but oh   it's too late.

'Never mind, Winner. I too am always late for everything. It never much matters in the end.'

The edges of the room encroach slowly, and shrubs and bushes appear, growing towards me. Drop of wine by my forehead, whiff of the sharp aroma, grapes, acid, cinnamon. Figures in shadow move around, along the walls that box me in. The lilt of laughter from my first wife – the one I'd really wanted to stay – I hear somewhere in the room.

Just as on the night we separated, 'Winner,' she says. 'You could take care of me but you won't and never did.' It took her hours to spit it out, or years. My heart full of brine at the sound of her voice, sinks to the ocean floor. 'Not enough, Winner, and then, and then.' Always the   and then. Her shirt orange, the colour of the tiles behind and the effort I'd made to light a candle, luminous her shirt sleeve but her face too dark, not enough of her to fill me. I was kept at the edge of hope, a sheer drop into nothing. I feel the emptiness still. 'Winner,' she says, 'you will be missed, but not in any of the important ways.'

Strange how the light towards the end of the day presses a change in my mood. Long light and shadows fold neatly around corners, two-toned rocks, branches

slick with under-shadow, pointed reaches of grass.
Hello family, pushing roots into the earth they settle
themselves here to keep me company. My closest friends
and children and grandchildren sprout from the ground,
just before my eyes melt. What shame. All throughout
my life, there were trees, shrubs, and without looking I
walked past.

'Never mind. All of this will go on existing. And I'm
done cleaning. I've cleaned your office for years, Winner,
your table and your lamp. You leave white powder over
the desk, I clean that. You leave cigarettes and brandy,
and the newspapers. I tidy that. You spill wine on the
floor, I clean it well as I can. You leave blood, I wipe it up.
And I keep wiping till it's all clean. Now you're naked.
Time for me to   drag this glutinous body into ground
waiting. The damp-licked, silent earth waiting. Time for
me to give your green-tinged mouth its lasting silence,
this body on its side, in the shape of a sand dune about to
be blown away.'

Yes, I see. As these generous shrubs and blades of
grass gather around, I am hopeful. Can't wait for the
ground to take me in, if I could, would haul me into
the ground myself, rake the dirt over myself in favour
of ground's sweaty cool, and I myself take root at last
I sprout. A single white root stretches downwards my
work for the day and I drink, and on the next day I reach
my green frond up to catch the sun in my palm and let go
this living for the lifeless, misery for blankness, created
for uncreated, and sound for deafness. Let go the phone-
bell's ring through which I, in the growing state of
death, speak to the living. And in this stone on my head,
beneath my name is written: There is a life in which I
was better. Ha. It wasn't mine.

BRIGHT SPACES

The cat's paws brush through the letterbox, looking for
some jellied meat or an opening in the family. Cat pushes
a letter through the door. The letter marked J.H. Ottessa,
dead brother of mine. My brother's bed sheets still
warm-sweaty. My brother's paw prints dented into the
doormat. Rainwater falls heavy from the gutter makes
me look up, makes me remember what day it is what
time it is. I call my little girl's name Annette A   eh
Annette A   eh voice through the wall, and the echo
of her name, Annette, from the other side. Her face
screwed up fingers in ears not to have to hear, Annette,
all the damn half-hour of the morning, of all the days to
be playing up the day of the funeral day late for church
day.

    But a child can grieve. Let the child be grieving, let the
child   be.

    Eight years old, were you Brother? And I a bit older. I
see you running down the street, a sun-blazed strip lined
with flowers begging for water, petals blown-out hearts.
It was a day with corn, heavily spiced and salted. Smoke
and charcoal. Nice. Heat beating a path into our bones,
our brows wet. You had a rug tied around your neck with
garden twine, lying out in the sun charge up charge up,
before flying off past the streetlight, past the telephone
wire, past the aeroplane. Almost choked yourself to
death. I stretched a hand out to you – hooked onto a gate
latch, the lynch mob's latest victim – to save you from a
strangling. You hit my hand away. And again. Something
in your eyes said this isn't a game. But I pulled you up,
pulled up out of the fire, that time, my hand melting into
yours.

    The church is cold. Warmed with bodies, they

sitting on they heels   huh   sitting in the dirt   huh
rocking on they legs, mouth open moans we perform the
wailing of the milk, mouths open red and glistening we
grieve, divide up the ashes, and return to our   leaking
gutters.

You were fifteen you were fine, then acting strange.
'Where's my outline?' you'd say on repeat, scratching
at the armchair as if it was a life raft. You alone in an
ocean, the deepdeep, 'You're rubbing me out,' you'd say.
'Don't tell me I didn't warn you, I warned you.' And we
couldn't touch you, you were so gone. Daddy shake you
by the shoulders, his wrists strong, finger-knuckles pale.
It was fear not anger made him act. Fear not anger made
Mother a quiet spot of light, a reflection on the wall.
    Just before, we had seen a cat at the side of the road,
struck dead in the morning's bending light. Covered in a
towel we lifted to see its face, jaw shut, eyes closed. You
were adamant that the cat, the beast, had taken a part of
you with it to hell.
    I'm closing your bank account. Looking for
details   details, a statement, a letter. Couldn't you have
kept this room in less disarray? Everything had its place
in your mind, sure, and now I'm sorting through your
memory bank of bird junk. Like our guttering stuffed
with leaves and debris, bottle tops, sweet wrappers,
not meant for the nest of a natural thing. Your hospital
letters and prescriptions all around here. Your bed sheets
warm-sweaty. Let me tell you, Brother, there's money in
that account, why did you spend so much time on the
streets when you could've been living something better
than you did? Doodles over everything: crabs walking
off the page, snakes eating their own tails, horseshoes,
kites a diamond divided into four, a lightning bolt

striking the letter X.

Thumbs-up was your best doodle. The white and pink of the nail a clean line, skin taut over the knuckles, a few hairs, the perspective so that the curl of the fist leant towards you. I saw you perfect that from the first year of school, to the age of university smart boy you came home with new words in your mouth, reciting the words like a humming prayer: vindicate, aurify, assimilate, quantum, divinity, ontology, petrichor, ossify, gravitation, explication, commodification, metaphysical, ad infinitum, fluphenazine, clozapine, and then quetiapine, pontificate, capitulate, and then exonerate, and then   and then   month on month your presence became an absence. Between your two eyes lay an open road. Yet you could explain to me that energy cannot be created or destroyed. The smallest fragments come together only to later be pulled apart and you, created, uncreated, one manifestation of a constant vibration from which you were formed and to which you would return. You were never really born and won't ever die.

So, you still have a key to the house, I haven't changed the locks. We're waiting for your return and we don't want you to be kept out in the rain. I can hear your tired hand knocking against the brass, a sharp intake of breath as you steady yourself, cursing, to find your way inside did I take enough care of you?

Once you said it was like walking through a door, passing from a dark room into another filled with a terrible bright light. In the corner of the room the beast would be waiting for you, coercing you to go deeper into the bright space, your position in the cosmos uncertain, held in place by a tense thread thin as the guiding line of a spider's web. I came to recognize the signs, 'Cat's creeping,' you'd say, 'I warned you, don't say I didn't warn you.'

Annette misses you. She doesn't talk about you much but holding her hand in the street I feel the pull of her recognition. Any bald black head in the street and she turns to you, your bald black head reflecting the weather, overcast or sunshine, or aurified with Sahara sand your big black bald.

A glass full of apple juice on your bookshelf, now on the floor in pieces. The carpet drinks it up. It shattered so easily, had a weakness. Picking up the shards of glass with my fingertips, and the vacuum, and I'm still here finding pieces stuck into the apple, nylon and dust, a sweet wheat – a smell like the sweat of the scalp. I soap it and leave the wet glisten to dry but the apple endures like a cloud in my nose. The books in your room endure, spines look back at me with indifference. The penned marks on your papers. Your alarm clock endures. Your bed sheets. The open window, the curtains and wind that moves them endures. Your big bald head endures, for us, endures.

I sense a warm charge in the air, precursor to a storm. How often does it rain in here? I think to gather up all your things before the rain thinks to wash them away. No, rain won't wash them away, holy water wouldn't wash us of you. When the rain comes, water will bounce straight off of me, bouncing off my oily feathers. A flock of geese fly overhead   through through my mind. It's a feathery mess I don't know how to clean up.

In the garden, the glut of rain has given the weeds new strength to reach for their sun. I've been worrying about the bluebells, and the Narcissus, yellow flowers. This year it seems like they might never come up and what can I do about it? I'm confined to a bubble in time, violet hues oscillate around my head, a metallic echo as I speak, my voice rebounds.

The birds are readying their nests. I've seen them around, busy with pieces of twig, plastic, grass, rubber, instinctive determination; instinctive, that's a word from your tongue. Your tongue in my mouth with the word, a fist uncurled with a gift. When I look into the eyes of the birds I see nothing but the dark. They don't need to try, to regret, no conflict in them to overcome.

Daddy cried in church. First time since he was a child, a guess. He didn't cry when his wife died, that's how I guessed. She had a story of her own but I didn't deign to hear it, didn't point my ears her way   no   NO the O is empty, the O symbolic (your word again) of a dark tunnel never travelled, an opening, Mother, I never entered. She a quiet spot of light.

Brother, you were the boy, seed of Daddy's back and brow, the boy of gold-turmeric-yellow as his left front tooth, yellow as that Sahara sand, everyone slowed to look at the sky a dappled yolk. That was something rare.

He will take your ashes with him back to the continent. To a tree of his own childhood. He will put your ashes into earth cracked like the wrinkles in your feet. Cracked earth, once mud, earth and water, earth and water with red hue like the rounded edges of your fingertips   huh   under a tree where the birds move in a line, making a hell of a noise as they jump from branch to branch.

Think of the smell of the earth, and shrubs of the bush dying away to make room for new green. Green the smell of early summer when Mother would cut our hair, me first because it was always a struggle. Daddy stretch out in the chair, best placed for what he has to say, what he always say. Home, talking of home. He never took us there. Home, talking of home and the ground, the colour of the earth, deep brown, red. 'Eat it, it make you strong,' he say. 'Earth pound by the fist of God   red hue   earth   crack like a rough hand   earth.'

My hair cut and fresh, I sit back and watch yours, your hair that grew faster, thicker. Watch the coils rain down onto the carpet like the spring shedding its feathered seed to the wind. Trust the immortal code find fertile ground. Trust it grow. Daddy going on, 'Listen for the sound of the forest at night, for the ancestor spirit, for the animal. Everything holy under the fist of God. Eat it, it make you strong.' Before relaxing into sleep, a whisky smile spread wider than his nose. His nose and the corners of his mouth draw an A, and his whole face says   ayyyy. You inherited the A nose, sturdy nostrils like round pipes, but you were beholden to the slim nose. You were unsatisfied. Yeah. And moody, lonely with your nose you blame for the girls look the other way.

We pounded our cereal into dust, God's pounded earth was the sand, the sandcastle his castle, pounded yams, grounded black beans and potatoes, chocolated powder; anything fine enough to squeeze through our fingers, or shudder through the air as dust. I see you lick the sweet dust from God's fist. I watch the spring fall from your hair, and sense the cool slice of Mother's comb. You raise your arms at this point. And I remember the rounded side of your face, the silhouette of a boy cut from a storm shadow of foreboding. The muscles in your back, as dents in sheet metal. Your eyes cut from the cold half-moon.

I watch you comb a beard matted from hours of disturbed sleep, white gown, wet fingers and Vaseline, the walls a faded yellow and a light grey floor

– impostering, lit so bright as to imitate whiteness. I help you rub a shine onto your head as you will the beast to be quiet. You turn to me in a clear moment and say, 'I always feel so lonely in these   bright spaces.' My eyes again fixed onto your silhouette, against the bright room you brown as browned with iodine, loved by a mother, repented by the father, grazed by faith   huh, was he?   canonized by the hieroglyph: the lightning bolt, the thumbs up, the kite (the diamond in four). 'Do you feel the cold?' you ask. I move around the room, closing the door and the windows.

From the church to our house there's a trail of ashes, memories that spill. Your ashes have lodged themselves beneath my fingernails, float on the draughts from room to room. They have a chokehold on me. Soon they will blot out the sun, the green will drain from the plants until all is muted, dead, and the earth becomes a wound.

But cheer me up, shit   tell me.

Every episode was a set-back.

A drug turned the beast into a pussycat, but made your limbs dumb.

And now the beast that haunted you will haunt me in the damp walls of the house, at work, in the light-hidden corners of every room, and pen-drawn lines striped by your hand which I may hold onto.

Annette has held onto more than your shadow, the child braver than I. Unafraid to look into your light that threatens to annihilate, and breathe in the dust of your bones. She can feel you in the damp corners of the house. Your words spilling from her mouth, vindicate, aurify, ad infinitum, forgive, instinctive, symbolic. Re-drawing the lines of your pictures, and the lightning bolt strikes X and Y. I should clean up the mess, throw the ashes, make it so that you're really gone. But rainwater won't wash you away.

Church had promised to wash away all that seemed wrong and disturbing; the payoff is on its way, from on high, be good. But it shrank from the unliveable, unsurvivable things – the beasts lurking, refusing to be cast out. Church is those people lost as anyone else, us who thought that through belief alone we could turn on the light, the bright. Yes. Electric bright lights installed, push away darkness to the faraway edges.

The split, church split, Brother, our family split that would someday land on your head, split apart from yourself, and us, and me.

And Mother knew something. She who on that warm Sunday morning raised her hands to the sky our Lord our Saviour, fanned her face with a folded paper, and doused her damp underarms with perfume, a heady musk that would betray to us a nervousness of this   church company. Singing the blues of less than belonging while Daddy shaking hands. You and me, fumbling with an elasticated tie, Sunday school, open your Bible, give not that which is holy unto the dogs, scratch of Velcro as you hook a foot around my ankle on that Sunday, holy day, good clothes day, good food day, smell the curry powder, chicken marinade, soy black as black, spring onions burnt sweet, skin roasts and fat leaks under heat radiating from Mother's palms. And we wait outside sit on the wall for Daddy to get the car and drive to that   chicken cooking, be good and you'll get dessert, past the estate and Daddy points out all those who weren't so blessed to be streets away from the sour tang of a piss stairway, how lucky we are.

I try to say something true. I don't have the vocabulary to say it. 'I am the way, the truth,' we would say sitting in rows can you hear it? A clash of memories, the only truth I can get at. And to love each memory without falling apart, to love is the hardest thing. My voice rebounds. Memory slips and is split, I disappear inside and everything else is lost because my brother, the good man is dead.

And still I can feel the breeze light on the arm hairs on that Sunday, good food day, play outside day, a bucket of water cold from the hose, my back jarred on the edge, head lowered into it like a heavy green paw paw with your hand a cradle, each finger a pulse into my scalp while you sermonize my being saved under Christ.

'Do you feel the Lord, son?' Your best southern states accent. 'Do you feel the Lord's nourishing dew?' Dew as in doo doo doo doo doooo, Stevie Wonder, tomorrow's mysteries are hidden from us who are here in the now. You told me I'd be saved today, 'Did the Lord tell you, did he tell you the news?' Did he as in Diddy Bop and Perseus built a staircase through the cosmos to the father of his birth to tell the truth, that he was not a star but a meteor, the song dropped last summer and did you hear it? You won't hear it.

You continue your prayer over me, lips pursed in a line, a steady hand, a scoop of water rained onto my forehead while your voice I hear, as if you're hidden over there where the bluebells supposed to grow, near drowned out by the thump O rain.

'Do you feel the cold?' you say.

My back-head is submerged and rush air into my lungs, cold rises up, pooling into an ache in my forehead, submerged again, deeper deep as my back can crane.

'Feel the cold water over you and the Lord's warmth will enter, and the light will enter and it will be blinding, and you will be good and you will surely receive the after-dinner cake.'

Submerged again and breathe   lungs deep, enter a room, close the windows. I hear a door shutting. The flap of a wing. Electric bright light.

'Blessed is your back-head as long as it's under water, blessed is your back-head as long as it's under. Do you feel the cold, Brother   ?'

Feel the cold   cold water.

GREEN AFTERNOON

A moan.

And I had to leave my chair, alone in the green   green afternoon.

The boy was bleeding from his side, eyes of gathering water   blind pools iridescent   lungs a well draining out of life   a gurgle deep.

My hand on his stomach (exposed with shirt pulled upwards where he had dragged the body across the slabs) and felt warmth and trembling and wet, blood sweats the wound.

'Young man,' I said, 'my man.'

His eyelashes fluttered, a moth caught between my fingers   flash   the life's out.

I looked behind me. As if nothing had changed, the sky, green green and the grass blue as ever, empty but for the chair, a book and a chair.

I dreamed of blood from then on. Oceans of blood, rains of blood. It wasn't fearful dreaming but was painful and true, like the fact of death, living under the shadow of it, and now I had two shadows curled up on me like a shell hard and no give.

Around the lawn there was tape. My street haze of blue lights. I was taped around my middle, property of the investigation, indefinite. The blood remained, marked as it had pooled, the shape of an arm I could make out, a ribcage young and taut. The clean knife in a bush over there, was his.

Investigation heavy, investigation clueless. How was he here, in your place? How did he get into your property one afternoon when you were alone in the green? A communal garden, excuse us, understood,

adjoined gardens private, still, you were the one to
witness. How was he in? That's unknown, officer, the
entry gate left unlocked most likely   must be a trail
of blood from where he laid himself down. I hadn't
deserved   the intrusion, officer, sitting with a book,
and then the moan, yes the moan, and then he sank into
the earth, leaving the pool of blood. My tongue is getting
thick, woman, can this end? Might need me again she
said, more questions. What's the matter with the answers
you've got, I said, my nose isn't long, it's only wide.

I sought counsel: a number to call, 'phone
consultation', appointment and   sit opposite him in a
chair, half-smile (not too much smile) and nodding at my
words and   to my annoyance   pencil grazing the
paper while I spoke.

'Blood in my dreams,' I said to the man.

'Getting any exercise?' he said.

'I could outrun a water buffalo, a zebra,' I said, 'I have
hooves man. What use is it though, to run about? With
no direction to go.'

At which point he looked down at my shoes, housing
what seemed to him obviously human toes. How stupid.
My eyes rolled in, I could no longer see, ears shrunk
closed. People blind and deaf to you will make you blind
and deaf.

At home. The plane trees in the green were bent
towards the site where   .

The police went quiet as cut grass in the weeks that
followed. I called to see if I could wash away the blood
stain. I was responded with a 'Who's this?' (Who the
hell is this? they mouthed, but their mouths so loud I
understood.) So I filled a bucket of water, Castile soap.
The stain now condensed to black, with water and soap

102

enlivened to red again and swallowed into the earth. The silence around the scene was unworldly, no fox squeal or chirp as is normal, heard my blood sing as it passed my ears.

'What for it?' a voice said to me. As tree and bush waved with the wind and branched   open arms. Some mercury in me expanded my veins and filled my mind, as if my own self was calibrated to that moment. 'What for it?' coaxing me again.

I'm going to find this killer and ask the right question then   and then have a why.

And from there (I'll say less by way of my deliberating, there was some) I took my hammer and nail to crack the shell, tapping for answers, beginning where the life had drained. My detective skills I took to be   as of yet undiscovered. If I were writing a note on this part of the story I'd call it:

¶ 1, death's power to invert all things

I photographed the site, on film, objects and edges blurry. But it wasn't precision I was after, not the faint details of the ground, but the mood.

How exactly had he entered? No matter, all I knew and needed to know was that he was here, the green space between the backs of houses.

I developed and pinned those images. One, the side-gate into the green. Two, my phone which I had used to call the officers, who did tape up and abandon me with the stain. Three, the site where   and the plane trees bent in mourning. Trees would recover, it was important to capture their bent backs as they were then, the beginning.

I looked in the local news, no ID of the boy too young. A picture of my street haze of blue lights. 'The victim had been...', 'The victim was found...', 'The victim was... liked,' from the middle pages. No capture, no one would grass-up, no one would give a lead and so the article ended with an appeal, and a full stop to say, 'We can all wash our hands clean'. But there was a quote from the mother, '- - - - - - - - - - - - - - - - -', as if she had risen from the pages and given me the first clue with her tongue, and what she clued was herself, and herself was to be found.

¶ 2, longest street marked by flowers

My street was the longest in the neighbourhood. Trees stand along it late spring to summer socializing, yapping their leaves.

I edged home one evening, all hat and suede and hands dry as chalk, grinding my teeth. Then noticed the flowers at the gate to the green. There were five bunches in all, of tulips, carnations and gladioli (or the sword lily, flowers in summer, unlike the tulip, but in many ways no more difficult to grow and should be planted before the last spring frost). I photographed each flower, and waited on my step for more mourners until just past sunset, none.

The next morning the flowers had increased by three, one pot of pinks in bud and bloom, peonies, white carnations. I looked closely at each flower in turn, there was a note, 'senseless' it said, but among it all no clue as to who the mother was.

I made a pot of coffee and with my book I sat on my front steps to keep watch, made sure to wave a casual

'Hullo' to any passers-by without giving away that I was
waiting for a flower bearer.

Night was quiet relief and in that deepest part, where
time slackens, the darkness stirred. A hooded mourner
made their way to the gate, sneaking soundless on white
trainers, with lilies, a human shape but beyond that I
couldn't make out, clothed in black and   oh   dark
glasses, so as not to be blinded perhaps, by the loss.

I stood, and cleared my throat. They froze, and raised
the glasses to look, slick of cheekbone and full lips,
eyes hooded in shadow. I expected them to run, my
hand gripped the step-rail like bird talons, but fattened
and fleshy, heartbeat at a decent pace, each muscle in
my back and legs and arms stiffened, tight from night-
ushered cold.

Glad for me there wasn't a chase, nothing in me that
was up to it. But I did walk down the steps cautiously, to
avoid breaking the peace between   us quiet figures
come down with the fever of spring.

'Could you tell me something?'

The flower bearer couldn't give the name of the mother,
didn't know. But led me on a path through the night
and   slick of cheekbone and full lips left me outside a
pub on the edge of an estate, coffee pot between my two
hands. Was she here in the drink hole? I suspected not.
I was cautious of provoking a reaction to my snooping
around. Hand pressed door and I was in, what was quiet
from the outside erupted into my ears filled with the
noise of people out late, so late.

There were those who slept on the benches edging
the room, 'We're not sleeping, we're dancing,' they said.
And those who filled the middle of the room in loud
conversation and singing to music and etcetera. I hid my

pot at the door. Tried to make my way towards the bar,
blocked at every turn, so I aimed my order 'Brandy and
coke!' towards the large ears of the ram serving.

My brother was a ram. His horns of bone-smoked
porcelain curled to the sides of his head like the parted
hair of Horace (the lesser known Horace, famed
for his middle parting). My memory of Brother:
fretting veins threading through his eyes, I imagine
that his vision was clouded with red-tinted light, like
the tint of every memory I have of him. These rams,
the curled horns feed pride-blown mouths, the instrum-
ent of their volatile temperaments, self-importance,
and   oh   sometimes, bravery, wisdom and honour.
Will this ram honour me with a drink?

It looked as though he would. A nod in my direction,
and then to another bartender (son of a worm) tall and
slinked his way along to the brandy, ice. Behind the
bar there was a long tank full of golden-orange fish
mouthing little Os in my direction. The ram and worm
too mouthed Os of viscous smoke as joint passed back
and forth. My drink was placed on the bar, and the ram
transferred to me his brown (animal feeling), and I grew
a chest width wider and found it in me to elbow my way
through, sipped the drink, placed my money on the bar,
beside the money I placed the photo of the site where   ,
and had my finger pointing his attention to the image.

He looked at it for a long while. I had finished the
drink. He had toked the joint the way through and his
eyes were red like my brother's, but he held a steady
gaze.

When done, gazed at me and said, 'Who is it pictured
here?'

'I thought you'd know, given the time you took—'

'You expect me to know the exact site where   , by

106

looking at a picture?'

'No – I suppose it was the length of your looking that made me—'

'You're looking for the person dead?'

'His mother, it was a boy too young for an ID. His mother gave a quote in the paper and said "– – – – – – – – – – – – – –".'

'Not much help. Could've been any mother.'

'I want to find who did it.'

'Who? Who?' Ram said, and laughed.

The tall worm chimed in, 'Who, who!'

My chest deflated, caved.

'Nobody will give you a who   man,' Ram said, 'you can roam around this estate all you like, ask your questions, make sure you're not known as police, is all we can say, and find the mother you're so keen to bother, you can't return her son.'

'But I was there when he   and can give her that.'

'Then go on. Come back when you know what we know.' Smoke thickened around his face and horns, crowd parted and my way through was given. As I left I grabbed my coffee pot, and felt I could go on.

'I can go on,' I said quiet to myself, 'now I can go on.'

¶ 3, Willow Walk

A side street called Willow Walk. I approached the estate it hummed the fluorescence of city asleep with one eye open. I'd forgotten what these places were like at night. No animal sounds here like at home (as is usual) not far away, but soon the concrete and brick took on the rough of bark, the bronze-green of moss combed by moonlight.

There was one light that flickered, I headed for that.

It was within a short underpass through one building, granting entry to a courtyard encircled by more, and more of them – buildings. As I passed beneath the flicker, the light went out. I was blinded, and the silence was blood again singing in my ears, heard someone exhale. Light on   flickering, at the end of the pass young man, two young women on a wall with heads bowed to talk.

I continued my step walked even. I tried too much I know, and held my body too normal I know, for a someone walking around a dark brick-lain forest at night.

In low light   their faces glow and shadow of youth, turned to me as I approached. The first, her hair in braids and one or two slipped from her shoulder as her neck twisted, and hung there touching her hand, and the other, lighter-skinned and pinch-nosed, almond eyes and hair slick back and pressed flat a single curl to her cheek, and him, a cap and hood up, and tall and dressed in dark, and slim, and also looking at me.

Innocuous, 'Good night, isn't it?' I said, 'I don't live here I'm sure you might have guessed. I'm looking for a family member, a cousin, who's recently lost her son.'

They spoke in sentences broken between three mouths, like a ball being batted between them and kept from touching the ground. 'So, cousin, who you asking for exactly? What's the name of your cousin and her son?'

I hadn't anything to say then. So I stalled and said that I didn't quite understand and could they repeat and they did, in a configuration different to the first.

'Who you asking for cousin exactly? So her son of your cousin? What's the name?'

I asked again, for the question to be repeated. And

they repeated without aggravation, and so I asked, asked, asked the question circulated their lips for   enough time for the moon to change position. I don't know.

'For asking name your cousin, what's and so you exactly? The son of who her cousin?'

At this point, to my shame and a fact I am myself unable to forgive, I wanted to turn back. My feet had absorbed the cold and I was feeling as if   made of paper or straw, my stomach had filled with coffee and not much else since before sundown. To pack in the mission for benefit of hunger's edge? Yes I was considering it. Has worse been done on an empty stomach? Yes. Have some men and women been given the chop in a cruel rush of hunger? And things said that cannot be unsaid? And knives thrust that cannot be withdrawn? Yes. My error was just to think and to carry on the thought until I was leaving that place the way I came and back up my steps and into bed to erase the night so far.

At the heart of things, myself   alone, feeling unable to effect any good. Waning belief let my mind adrift on the winds of pale satisfactions, rumble in my stomach, my dining table, sitting, warm feet. The people in the pub didn't believe in the good. The death wasn't my fault, it wasn't. But the animal-headed people would have laughed if I'd stopped then, even if I never went back I would've heard them laughing on, and these three young ones went on and on. Until they arrived at a question I could answer.

'What's your cousin? The cousin name? Exactly who so asking you for her son?'

'My cousin is a man, son of the brother of my mother. The name, Bartold. The mother, in the newspaper, asked me for news of her son, who died at the site where   , and so died with me,' I said.

They responded, again between their three mouths, I caught the sentence I wanted to hear. It was Jahona I needed to find, Lucida Court, near the only tree in the estate.

Walking in the direction I guessed was right, water drop   onto my hand, dots onto dry skin and into the coffee pot, top up the dregs, light rain became heavy. I stopped in another underpass, my feet stiff with cold and ache, shoes becoming hard-soled and tight on the arches. I sat down, my back to the wall, and sipped at the coffee propped the pot by my side   listen   to the sour brown lapping at the glass pot with metal rim, keeping this rhythm that I call time.

Rain fell long, stretched threads of colour-white. The moon blindfolded in cloud. Found a mint in my pocket and ate. Through the patter I heard the regular brush brush of a tense broom, balcony on my left side and a woman brushing up and down the walkway. Up high. Crazy as. Like my ma, sometimes her arms are still up to it, sweeping the walkway on a balcony not dissimilar, where she keeps her flowers (and taught me the flowers), sweep of the broom regular with the sureness of night and day, sure as my brother coming home with a punch in the shoulder for me, wound up from a day doing whatever he did with his friends on the streets.

And likening this woman to Ma, how she sweeps, following some internal rhythm is how I got to this place? Brush brush, tiny papers fell from the walkway, then blown about and wetted, some bunched up in corners, and carried then further by quick swirls of wind. Those papers, I imagined one or two of them holding the names that I was missing, the boy, the killer, and with my mind nearly a blank sheet of white, my chin nodded to my chest, eyes closed.

¶ 4, just a head, light and cleared of thoughts

I felt the sound before I heard the sound. Rain had
petered out, giving the air a crispness. And through the
wall, and through my arse on the ground I felt a bass,
deep, made by some other-world animal? A thought that
was confirmed, a pair of eyes to my right, fixed on me
with the clarity of the fresh-after-rain.

To my feet. Woman was sweeping still. Shook off the
grog and paper that had gathered at my side, all blank,
if they ever did have names. The eyes glowed red with a
light that filled my own eyes, was all I could see cleared
my thoughts, cleared my body away I felt my arms and
legs disappearing. Enticing. Surpassed my urge to stay
hidden. Without arms and legs, without a body I   just a
head   moving forwards, no bodily fears, as all my fears
were subsumed into the red, and no pains therefore.
The bass was something akin to music, like none I've
ever heard and closer I got to the source I saw objects
emerge: red at first with faint lines, then darkening to
firm silhouettes, boxes piled on the ground, door frame
and open door, feet, arms, hands, necks, heads, noses put
together into figures moving, slicking back and forth at
work, at this hour?

Big men, shoulders enormous, forearms long and
lined with ink, or scars, no heads hunched from heavy
work and slow dragging bodies, but heads high, and
mouths moving? Yes. One even blew a plume of smoke
from his mouth while standing, back towards me,
head turning left and right, a hand in his pocket he
seemed relaxed as anything. Them shifting little bags of
something up a stairwell was the reason for their walking
back and forth with intention.

Closer I got, these big men getting smaller, and now

I was closer than five metres and they were not men but boys, and some girls on the periphery, all shrunken in stature before me. Their skin in red light was so soft looking, and they became younger and younger, these babies' plump lips poked out, cheeks fattened, and a sweet smell wafted from them, like mashed, overripe apples.

The baby with head turning left and right caught sight of me, the lookout. I heard a howl, or cry, or moan, a call to assemble it must have been, because then they all did join the first, increasing in number, five, eight, thirteen, around a fire of red eye   car lights, steady on low, smoking engine, and heat exuding, deep bass a growl like I should call it mother. As I was surrounded, felt my body   suddenly   too keenly, who was I kidding coming here all arms and legs? I shrank myself in as much as I could, they scratched at my chest, neck and face until I bled, and clumps of my hair I saw falling past my face as the plump-lipped babies drew and drew blood. I threw myself to the ground, whipping the contents of my pot into the air as I went, enough commotion for them to stop a moment and for me to say, 'I'm not police, none of my business what you're doing, looking for Jahona.' And it was tense quiet for a while.

I had courage enough to open an eye, sit up, and open the other. The pot had cracked like a scar across the face, but not broken and I hugged it in, and saw raised scratches across my hands throb and ooze.

'Jahona's at Lucida Court,' one said, finally. 'And you can't sneak up on mans at work and expect it to go well.'

'Fair,' I said, 'I'm her cousin.' But didn't mention the boy for fear of the reaction. 'Could you point me the way?'

'We're moving that way, so wait.'

I stayed sitting. They searched every part of my person until they were satisfied I was civilian, and returned to the work. There were others moving around them to buy some of the stuff, figures emerging from light and car exhaust and shrinking back into some groove of their own. They sold that   I guessed, I didn't say out loud even in my own mind. And one by one they sat and rested tired next to me, and perhaps because of my benign status, they talked.

Baby, sitting to my left, in green shirt, wore a studded chain with wings, proud to show himself pictured on his phone, a pose with jagged knives, hood up, showing it off for what? I asked.

They talked of the hunt, 'When we were young,' they said, and I, incredulous, knew that they couldn't have gotten any younger now and still be able to stand on stiff legs, any younger and they would have flopped over, rolling rubber-like on the ground, their talk turned to babble, any more again and they would have been returned to the fragile plane of the unborn, skin dissolved, each soul a tiny candle burning open to the air   risk of being snuffed out by the sigh of a moth's wing, or an old man breathing through his whiskers.

'When we were young.' Opposite me, with cigar burnt down to a stub, continued. 'There was this boy, yeah.' And I said nothing, was this the boy I was here on behalf of? 'Robbed one of our boys, coulda been worse, but he and his had to know we don't mess around.' He held me by the eyes as he spoke.

'He was your enemy? And his boys?' I said.

Some laughter then.

'All a dem, except for the ones in here. And even then.'

We sat by car light with bass vibrating through

our bones, holding us there to the floor. I began to understand some small bit.

'This place, you protect?'

'This rock, this mud, this earth,' they said. 'We keep order and fairness.'

'Revenge is the rules,' baby in green shirt said, 'one day, caught sight of the boy on road, luck, got us-selves together real quick, real gassed, real hyped, on bikes, and got around looking for him, found him hiding behind a wall.'

A burst of laughter from all of them, high and short.

'And then?' I said.

'He ran, of course.'

'You caught him?'

'Nah, the bus ran him down innit. He ran into the road and the bus ground him down flat.'

'You can't spend your time just doing that. Messing around with the order of things,' I said.

'And you're doing serious work around here? What are you doing round here?' The only girl to speak, pointed her finger at me.

They laughed. Howling laughter that was more and more a howl and more animal-like they seemed to me, in the red. Sharp noses attuned to sniff out each other, the mood of the street, or stale rhetoric and promises of regeneration generation over generation – it was a mournful howl.

Now was the moment. 'And, Jahona's son?' I said, and muscles tightened around the pot still in my arms. But they didn't hesitate to say:

'Our man, he was our boy, one of us.'

And I left a space without speaking, in the hopes of drawing more out of them.

'Don't know what he was doing in those ends, though,

they found him behind rich-people houses. But he had links all over innit. We'll know soon who did it, truth is round the corner, under every brick and stone. When we know who, we'll deal with them.'

He was their man, their boy. Boys are men, boys and men. These howling babies like a wolf pack, long-knived and short in the tooth, they did pack together and fit like pieces of a puzzle, like the network of roots that allows the tall tree to withstand the rush of a storm, the palest of winter droughts, the long dark nights of half-sleep without a coffee pot, indebted to the growling wolf mother, and each a father to each.

¶ 5, too late to see them

Me and my body, and the babies, began walking in the direction of Jahona. I was part of the pack for a short while, and felt the loose ends of invigoration, long forgotten, in the deep cavern of my belly, where somewhere a candle still burns a flush of youth and rage. I could see the tree on the approach, a birch so quiet, no yapping as is usual for a tree between blossom and leaf-bloom, no anticipation of what's to come, as if stuck between seasons' stillness without time.

A yellow flower at its foot, I grabbed it from the ground, dirt and roots in hand (Narcissus, to root us deeper into hope).

From a dark corner came someone, with hand out and searching for a fix that we   they   could provide. And one of the pack went off into the dark to provide, before a shout clenched the air around my ears. I saw them, and more and more of them, there were police undercover and more police emptied from the hidden corners onto us.

This isn't how it's supposed to go, I'm told, don't make your sale right where you all stay, and while together. We felt too safe, and were sloppy. Undercover police. It was too late to see them, too late to dodge them. My presence I   guilt over it.

One of the police came direct at me and politely requested my talking to him.

I began to sweat.

'A few questions, to follow up,' he said, as if we were acting a different scene from the rest. Over his shoulder I saw   babies dragged to the ground, one by one, and one tackled by two police, with elbow bent behind him then leaned into the ground by their knees, those blunt instruments, and barking from the shadows, teeth and glint of wet black eyes. They howled the last   night-time gong. I dropped to my knees. Babies fled from this mud and earth they protect so much, or after faces pressed into it and munching enough grit, pushed into vans waiting, off to their cells. Two police stayed behind with me and I was ushered to a seat on some stairs. Coffee pot clutched and wouldn't let go now. Something divine about the vessel   wouldn't let go. And they asked, again no new questions but more of the same, never mind how I came to be in this place tonight, with babies. But questions for some self-satisfaction for them, that I could not grasp, answers I could not provide. And how was he *in*? What was he doing in the property   sir when you were alone in the green?

I was back again. In that afternoon, sky and grass   as ever. My sad book flat at page open facing up. And I sat in the chair, but could not embody the Me of that day, oblivious to everything that was to come next, and everything that was happening on my street, and streets away. But I've never been carefree exactly. There was always the tiny candle that could blow this way or that. I put a hand to my breast where I was keeping the knife that had dropped to the ground in the raging and chaos just before, to save the babies some bit of trouble. Beneath the handle a patch of sweat. I felt my fear more keenly, as prickles up my spine when the cool of the blade caressed my shirt, jagged edge scratch as the blade caught the fibres.

Hand on my shoulder. Hard stairs and smell of rain and rust. The police retreating. 'More questions   later.' Left alone I looked up, numbers, a list of names and buttons to call, Jahona, 65 A.

¶ 6, paper covered with the missing name

I pressed the button, buzz and click, firmly pulled the door open, up the stairs enclosed in glass held by a metal grid painted cobalt blue, reached the flat, knocked, door like weightless opened under my fist, a step in cautious, my scratches had dried but still throbbed.

Inside, a corridor, L-shaped. I followed it round to the left, dark, and light on in just one place, the kitchen. There she sat under single light hanging and curtains closed (remain closed night and day). It was her, Jahona, sat at kitchen table, hair tufting from beneath a scarf, dust bustling around hanging light like a cloud of restless insects.

'Thanks for coming,' she said.

'You don't know who—'

'People coming night and day, a blessing, sweet night and day.'

Her mouth curled, serene, and her eyes wrinkled

with kindness, but was the kindness of yellow flower
drooping, as her gaze never met mine, always looking
just below   below my eyes.

Me, unworthy visitor, dragging my scratched body up
there to give her nothing but news of nothing, and her
boy's death, she already knew. And a vow to catch the
killer – no effect on that so far.

She said she wanted to show me his room, back out
into the corridor, her hand patting the wall for the light
switch, on, and walls filled with pictures of the boy,
as young and even younger than he was that day, in
school uniform and smiling, year on year. The corridor
had three more doors coming off it, all of them closed,
and from the ceiling hung streamers, bunting, deflated
balloons, like willow, vine and moss, in colours red, blue
and green.

She opened the door ahead of us. In there, clothes
folded on shelves, the best clothes hung on a rail ironed
shirt and trousers, bed, pictures on the wall – places
wanted to go, his friends – and behind, it all opened out
to a field, hiss of the wind-grass bending to the east, and
swaying trees in a line much further away as the field
broke into a wood. A noise to break the silence of this
place, and a clock on the boy's side table   ticking a
noise too.

'What is all this doing here?' I said to her, no answer,
her back was turned and walking out. I followed, shut
the door to his room, closed now to promise of the new.

'You have other children?' I asked.

'No,' she said. And edged the corridor, slowly,
with one hand always touching the wall and the other
pointing my eyes to the photographs and telling me his
age in each, seven, four, thirteen, skin radiant of camera
flash, of light, and a smile brilliant teeth. He was tall, I

118

knew, popular with girls, and difficult to reason with, and messy with his room, she had tidied it most recently, and had been sleeping in there since he'd been gone. She didn't mention the field of grass, or trees.

I asked her if she had been exploring in there, she responded, 'Where's there to go? To explore, I can't, I can't expect anything new. Nothing of newness there for me to witness, can't see no green, only blackness made by this still time, can't leave these rooms and corridor, no forward or back, past and future was ripped away, and I'm bound to this silence. Maybe it won't be always, but it is now.'

Once close enough I cracked the door to his room, to double-check my faculties, which I had begun to doubt. The grass was there, enough to smell it, yes. I entered the room, taking her hand, past the bed and beneath my foot the crunch of grass but I felt her resist. She wouldn't go any further, her face, there was no curiosity in it, no recognition for solace, green and sounds offered by this secret field. Out of respect I didn't push, but crouched and took the flower from my pocket, shoved it into the ground. Its stem was blue, blue of the sky blue, in contrast to the green field. I shouted 'Goodbye!' and heard my voice disappear into buffer of open space, air, trees and breath of the wind, colours and sound as such, where I'd always known them to be.

The kitchen table. I told Jahona that I had a hand on him at the end. And that his young soul was sunken somewhere into the earth of the green, behind the backs of houses. The trees were bent towards the site where   he had died. Her eyes met mine for the first time, and were not smiling now but contained an ocean's depth, and water filled their edges. A bowl of oranges on the table, released sweet-acid smell of ferment. She had a paper clipping in front of her, I held out my hand, she gave. The local story, my street full of police, Jahona quoted, 'Identifying the body of my son, I looked into the face of silence,' and written across in pen repeated, his name.

She heaved in sobs and my insides sank like a stone into water.

'I'm sorry,' feeble, from me, 'I looked for answers and I've found none. But I will collect, if I may, what you have told me in tears.' I held the coffee pot out to catch her tears and it filled to the top.

¶ 7, whosoever makes the word, ends the game

My feet would hardly bend to carry me out of that place. Out of the flat, the estate. Was I tired or just weighed by   unease, that heavied as the night went on? Jahona didn't know who had killed her boy, not even a name or nod in the right direction – the police thought that she was holding back. 'I wouldn't hold back a thing,' she had said. She had nothing to lose now.

A pot of tears. Sat my arse on a wall on Willow Walk, hand in my jacket to find a tissue for my brow and grasped the knife a second. Electric feeling in my palm and fingers. The danger was over, but I sweated no less.

I went to the pub, hand pushed door and inside people much subdued, ceiling full of smoke and low talking in a stupor. The ram was seated at a table to my right, and caught me in his eye just after I'd caught him in mine, and, 'Ahh he's back,' from him, and others then turned in my direction, tugged at my sleeves to guide me to a seat. Ram's arm around my shoulders, heavy, my back hunched under it.

120

'So tell us what you found out,' he said.

'Well, I found his mother and told her that her boy wasn't alone when he went, and named the location where the trees lean over the grass and—'

'Some cold comfort for a mother then.'

'Yes.'

'And the killer, you caught him or her and strung them up?'

'Nothing on that, nothing.'

'It's not so easy is it, detective?'

'You said I'd find it out, what you already know.'

'First, you can join our game.' Grunts of enjoyment from the worm, and other men and women, passing around a joint oozing smoke. I wanted to drag myself out of there. Not play. The pot I'd left tucked at the door was a pinch on my mind.

'Can you turn my smile into tears?' he said.

Again like my old body on the stairs earlier that night, I stiffened in my mind and nothing came. How to make a ram cry? I recounted how I'd found the boy, details, how he'd moaned and tried to say a name or something while holding my gaze through water in the eyes. I said to them all   how warm the blood. How it had pooled   so much of it, it might have formed a tide, and then it had darkened to black, and since then I am submerged in this black and quiet night.

But he stayed smiling. I beat my fists on the table and hung my head, looked up and locked eyes with a fish in the tank, felt its gaze on me and mouth an O pulsating, round eyes and narrow face watching, while people around me puffed out smoke in similar motion.

I had it. I went to the door and picked up the pot, put it in the centre of the table so everyone could see.

'Your tears,' I said, and stood back.

'Your pot is cracked,' he said, and gestured to my clothes and to the table where the pot, half full, was leaking onto it, and had emptied onto me. I must have smelled quite strong of body by now, sweating still and desperate for an answer, to leave soon. The electric feeling spread from my hand, across my torso, into my neck and eyes, and agitating.

'That's right, laughing is all you can do, a tear has never left that face!' My dejection only invited more laughter, punishing eyes of fish.

'Whosoever makes the word, ends the game,' he said, 'I start with a smile and end in tears.'

I was ready to throw myself at him, but I noticed, just next to where he was sitting, paper pieces, each with one letter of the alphabet, A, B, C, O, X and so on. Amongst them the word 'smile' was spelled out. I hovered over the papers and then changing one letter at a time moved towards the wanted word. And talked out loud to help me through it:

'I start with a "smile", along the footpath I move and climb over a "stile", no animal, no ram or worm can follow me, on the other side I step on a pile of "stale" manure and over the hedge, a ram locks me in a "stare" with no sympathy for my bad luck, in his eyes he possesses the "stars" and I, drawn by animal feeling, enter his eye screaming, I'm thrown towards the sun which "sears" my skin, my eyes burning full of "tears".'

A rush of relief, opened something in me, short-lived.

They all got to their feet. I grabbed the pot, holding in whatever could be kept in with my hand. Felt the leak of tears over fingers.

'You had a fun night roaming around with the boys, I'm sure. Tell us what we already know,' Ram said.

At last I said, 'If I want a pot to be cracked, I throw it

to the ground.'

They clapped furiously, breathed out thick smoke. I coughed, and as I coughed out of my mouth flowed yet more heavy smoke, stung my eyes, full of water and itching stinging, spilled whatever was left in the pot onto myself.

Back again. In the green back again. He was standing beneath the plane trees that weren't bent but tall   again, stretching to the sky dark and pinked with clouds, I could see well. My clothes and body damp with sweat, tears, and in my agitation (electric feeling) lurched for the boy and took the knife from my breast and shoved. Drove it in. Pulled it out and   jagged edge ripped out sinew after sinew like feathers from fowl.

He fell. A moan. This rock, this mud, this earth and run.

I ran through the back door of my house and out of the front, down my steps and street haze of blue lights and tape. And myself stunned. I ran with eyes wide, street studded with mourners and grievers and mothers and police, their round eyes looking back at me, mouths open glistening red, and faces contorted with surprise, mouthing the little Os.

there is no meaning. Hanging a picture on the wall
I   give   a little too much force to my thumb skin
breaks under pressure an orb of blood   red   red to
dark red   to dry red   to skin   to iron   to rust   to
heat   to sweat   to yesterdays as we move, we move.
Tuesday. Going into the city with the rest of them sliding
down the greased pole of means become ends. Let me
tell you. I slipped and travelled against the sharp grain
of escalator, one flight of metal before I hit flat floor and
crack, to the back of my head. I cried like a child oh I oh I
said me   am in pain.

    I was at work by the afternoon. At home by early
evening feeling burning scratches on the backs of my
legs and the bruised curve of my head. My mind curved
bruised.

    In bed, the sheets scraped and tugged me sore any
way I tried to lie. I   face down, looking for a cool
place, stretched out an arm and all that was solid
dematerialized. I   a nothing slipped into water. Water,
as pressure. I felt the water as pressure. I'd always
thought of pressure as a pushing down   oh   it was
every drop of water for miles working into me. There
was nothing to my fingers, no weight, no force on the
pads of my feet, no cold draught wafting past the hairs
of my skin, no sound, no sight. I couldn't set my watch
to nothing. I waited, couldn't scream, unaware of mouth
or lungs to do so not breathing, not dead, not alive. No
fear. Not yet. Eyes wide open into dark and no sense.
Unsayable.

The Friday, I dropped in on Uncle Padana. It was early
summer: shadows fold neatly around corners, light

warms the backs of the hands until four and cools before six. He answered the phone in a lady voice as I stood outside his consulting room, buzzed me in, He's ready for you now. He was sitting behind his desk, leaning back in his chair looking boyish, expectant, tired. A Ceropegia hung from the bookshelf and fondled the few hairs on his head. As I moved into the room he stood and for me opened his arms.

I told him about the fall, the senseless black of that night. He cupped the bowl of my head in his hands, throbbing sore into his palms.

'What painkillers you on?' he said. He speaks out of the side of his mouth – gritted teeth, broke his jaw, never set right.

'Something weak,' I said.

'Do you feel weak, sick?'

'Nothing.' I cupped my elbow rough pad, a graze dried red, and the other elbow, the same.

'A crack to the head. Confusion, no doubt.' He took away his hands.

'Confusion isn't the feeling,' I said, 'and you were there, and cousin Rhumz was there.'

'Was I kind?' Scratching a nail over the stubble above his lip.

'Kind?'

'Pleasant, agreeable.'

'You weren't there in your physicality, at least, too dark to tell.'

'No light to bounce off my face?'

'No light to see.'

'Black?'

'Deeper than black, than basalt, as deep as death. You were a presence, not yourself.'

'Well, take a light next time–'

'If there's a next time.'
'Yes, then I might know that I was kind to you.'
'You are.'
'I want to know if I am, truly.'
'You're serious?'
'Look around.'

I looked. A yellow corduroy sofa. The long list of
clients whose arses had worn it down talking it out for
the cure, a stack of them stretching up to the crows.
To the left, a wall of books. The wooden floor, with a
walking path where varnish was worn to the wood.
Piles of paper. Three pairs of glasses. The room was a
rectangle. That plant was the only plant. Us three the
only living things in the room that I could see. The
things I could not see: mice beneath the floorboards,
dust mites, woodlice work their way into gaps come out
at night. A bowl of oranges, living or dead, I couldn't
decide. A window. Outside, a high wall, over which
street life ran along as water runs downstream.

'I'm all about your night visits. You tell me, you tell me
everything.'
'Okay.' I hugged him.
'Rest your head dear, lie horizontal. I worry.'
'I will.' Out of the room.
'Call your sister?' he said, as the door closed behind
me.

We were eleven when our father died. Sunday
morning and I reached for my phone, touched her name
and let it ring, no answer, but I felt she was at the other
end watching it ring. A petty satisfaction I had then I was
petty, pleased because she was so petty. Our blood was
separated at birth but still runs hot through both of us.
There was no big feud, that would be too easy, simply,
we both need the upper hand. Our father died   he

died. Twenty years of hot friction have passed since then. He cooled the blood. He waved the flag to signal the end of the race. He's dead. We found no way of being without him.

That night, I took the bedside lamp, an arm outstretched from the sheets.   Light in my hand to extend my gaze solid shield against darkness. My hand backlit glowing. I pointed the lamp downwards, illuminating my feet, thighs, chest, arms, all there. It was snowing. Watch it fall through the lamp beam. Then I was afraid, and the cuts on my legs did burn then. The light would only penetrate a metre in any direction, and beyond that a void contained me. Last time being there I was a nothing, now, myself and body entirely oh   shone light in a circle around while the white stuff fell into darkness beneath me. Arm moving against dense water, resisting. I   floating   an obstacle in the snow's path. It settled into the hollows of my collarbones and attached to ragged braids of hair, but I couldn't feel it. It weighed nothing.

I wrote everything down after then: the pressure, I'm becoming accustomed; time undeterminable; snowfall, grey-white, like pieces of bleached moss; presence of Padana like hands cupping my head, Rhumz a tickle at the top of my throat and eyelids, as if singing a high note; no sighting of a living thing   yet   no skin and bone other than mine yet. That fear carried on in me, dread of emptiness all around and no way to go.

Some research at The Gross Library. I looked for oceanography and geology, cruised the pages of *The Silent World*, *The Deep*. I'd travelled deep, so deep, I knew that. My cousin, Rhumz, had been the librarian at The Gross for years, until she had the kids. I'd catch her in the toilets sometimes, mouth open red glistening, brushing her tongue in the mirror. My habit of going to The Gross stayed after she left. I sat at library desk with head propped on my hand let thoughts run through into evening. Through the window, a streetlight, a fox inside the light's yellow triangle, looking up, tipping back its head, black-tipped ears folding back, dipped ink black, catching yellow falling from the streetlight. Then gone.

At home, I picked up the phone. I said, 'You were with me last night, Rhumz.'

She said, 'Ha, sweetheart. Where was I last night? (Voice quieted as she turned to bring in her husband.) I was cleaning some five-year-old-child gunk out of the U-bend, wasn't I?'

'Yeah,' he said.

'What else will they find for their fun and games? The dangers of children, the perils of living with children. It's us who need protecting, cousin, it's us who are naïve, cousin. How could I have been with you?'

I said the same thing that I'd said to Padana, though Rhumz was a different temperament, a different grain.

'Presence? Well fuck me, I've always wished I could be two places at once. But I never was there, not me. You know one of them left a little nugget of something at my front door, on the mat. They think they're all cats and dogs and little elf people. The kids think they can be anything they want. Leaving little shits over the mat. I'm a cat or a dog they say, and that works for them. Cousin, don't let them fool you, the perils of family life it's too late for me. The party's over after a point. It's all old cigar stubs from then on. How's your sister?'

After Rhumz, I called Sister again. Again, no answer. Had I finally put her off? There were only a few axes of love, hate, attention in this world to sustain me, Padana,

Rhumz, and Sister – Grindy. She was where?

I never got very close to Grindy. Voice at the end of the phone, sometimes. Voice from across the table. Face at the other side of a grave. Wet eyes returning my gaze. I'd always fancied that her back was covered in acne, warts, moles with roots deep into the heart of her.

A fantasy close to me at this point. I, small as a flea scaling her back, looking for a foothold such as a protruding mole, ingrown hair, pimple. I reach the base of her neck, she screws her head around to look at me and I fall, scream with no sound.

I poured a glass of vodka, warm, and paced. As I passed the bookcase, a spike of pain. A small shard of glass lodged in my foot, a fresh wound to join the others. I washed it out with some drink, dabbed it with a tissue and drank more and sat down one minute and the next, I was in the snow. My lamp, shining right at me, suspended about a metre in front, glass in my hand.

The snow was dead matter, faecal matter and inorganic matter. Over weeks it falls from the ocean's surface to the deepest layers. A tug at my foot. Sharp teeth, a tail, something that liked my blood. The first time feeling something here. Oh   I felt the teeth sharp in me and I liked the feel. I'll say it again I liked it. The pink eel rasped at my foot, coiling itself and flexing, tugging, eyes black as the surround. I flicked my foot and it held on, my heel fresh meat to chew, so I kicked downwards, harder, and it let go. I followed it with my lamp beam as it undulated, body S-shaped light and shadow. I moved, as if running, fanning my arm out behind me downwards   downwards through the snow now only the eel I had for company. And Padana and Rhumz I sensed in the dark.

The eel led me to a pool, I examined it piece by piece.

A blue lagoon encrusted at its edges with smooth, charcoal-black pebbles, a slick mist of ochre hung above it. The eel disappeared into it and never reappeared into my light. Water beneath water? Dead crabs and eels lined its edges. The black pebbles, at a closer look, were mussels, mouths open, ready to swallow me oh   terrifying and so   beautiful it has to be seen unsayable beyond I know. I put my feet onto its surface and felt it push back. Wisp of blood from my heel drift away. To feel my feet. I didn't have feet before they had something to stand on. A surface. Now my feet were accustomed. Unsteady though   it was   unsteady the surface could have swallowed me.

A red light. Legs kicked I held the lamp with one hand, plug dipping into the lagoon. I followed the red light, just like the eel moved, undulating my legs as if they were swinging ropes and I drifted forwards so slowly at first it took time. But there was so much time   I'm getting used to it. Closer to the red, I pointed the lamp. Teeth transparent pincers, eyes glancing to its sides – foil dishes – as its dagger head cut through dark water. It travelled without fear, red light beneath each eye, for lighting the way? That hinged mouth. It didn't hurry away from me. I followed and forgot for how far or how long we burrowed into dark, me and this fish. A long swim through the deepest layers. Long swim through the snow into the nothing beyond sight lines overhead. And pool after pool, haze beneath my feet. Overhead there were bioluminescent pathways. And mine, my lamp beam, my red-light fish.

I followed the fish into morning. The vodka had spilled onto my lap. Head jerked back over the sofa arm, dried spit on my chin. My foot was red, dried blood, the glass cutting not so deep. But the memories of the glass, too deep, my heart of lead.

He had been sitting here one night, though I had
taken back his key. He'd been sitting here naked one
night. Light on he stood, dry skin, scratched and looking
sore, limp penis, which he put in my hand. Limp like a
soaked cloth. It was I who'd limped him, he'd said.
I held on to the penis. In part because it was warm
and my hands were cold and shaking. For old times'
sake   then. The glass was thrown later. In the struggle.
The glass was thrown to give me time to run away. To
give me time to run and to find the edge. I changed the
locks after a few   days.

Malacosteus niger. The fish can be found in the
midnight zone, with a flashing red cheek for attracting
prey. Though its nature not as violent as its teeth.
It was an ugly companion, leading me further than
I'd have dared to go alone with just the lamp light.
Synaphobranchidae, the eel that ragged my foot for the
taste of blood. The lake was filled with brine, a cold seep,
salt deposits from sea after sea, leaching out from below
the bed. An ochre haze of bacteria floating above it, thick
cloud of cells a soup wants to be left alone undisturbed, I
know I understand. I knew its surface in the sense of my
feet.

Leaving the library that night, I walked down the fox's
alleyway, past that lonely streetlight, fried chicken
bones. Once out of its beam I waded through that pink
city darkness. As I walked along dark alley black shoes
dipped into tarmac. Legs swinging black. Feet kick
through black. Only I could really know what I'd seen.
I would speak with Uncle Padana, as he'd asked, hear
his pencil burning at the other end of the line he'd go
quiet, cooking up diagnoses, feebly, but in true he was

132

stumped. I called Sister again a few times, again nothing. Thick air between us.

I should have known that she would show up the next time. Unlike the others she was there in the flesh. Unlike me, she looked dead. Her skin yellow, as always, but pale, above us a ceiling of flashing fish cruised along, her hair in thick bulging soft braids which wafted around her face, obscuring, reappearing, and she was silent. She was dressed the same as me. She always dressed the same as me – that was something I hated about her. Hated her ability to dress. The only difference was that she was wearing shoes, Mary Janes, black front buckle. I moved closer to my sister. Her feet and hands were puckered. My face inches from hers, her eyes were open staring ahead into the lamp, brown irises illuminated. Then she blinked, slow. Mouth opened and closed, mechanical, like a young bird begging for food. The eyes moving but no fixed gaze. Her limbs and head floated, drifting with the currents. I moved to touch her, but I couldn't. My hand a weight, her puckered feet in my eyeline. I was alone. I swivelled my lamp about me, I was close to the bed. Tube worms, red-lipped, floral, spread like grass beneath me there was no room for standing.

I've seen an eel tie itself into knots, poisoned by the brine. I'd shone my light on it. Grindy's eyes had seemed empty as the eel's. She was retreated deep inside, so deep her body was just another floating debris fallen from the surface, eyes opaque as the brine pool. The eel's head had jerked back and forth – the crack of a whip. It was momentarily surrendered to a powerful terror. Body a black stone underwater. But it did survive.

After then, my travels down the tube rails seemed the stranger thing. Travelling into the city with the rest of them, sliding down the   . Eye contact eyes snap away. The city demands a certain kind of contact only. It demands suspicions. Changes the meaning of a glance or a look of love, to yourself you keep your looks only to your own chest. It begins with everybody and nobody. People   flashing lights they   shoes, make up, rats' tails and so on   hinge-necked   bulb-headed bug-eyed. We are all alike in this strangeness. But I was accustomed to the dark pressures of the water oh   I'm no longer accustomed to this.

Last time. I was at the edge of a trench. At the edge, lamp in hand. Trying to see into it there was no point. Legs kick into black. I shone my lamp into the trench, but the light was swallowed. No point in the lamp light, too deep. I turned, they were all there. Everywhere I shot a beam there was Padana, Rhumz with Husband, the kids, getting on with things: moving rocks, feeding the tube worms, corralling the few fish into neat groups according to size, colour and temperament. And I was grateful, but I had to go.

I circled around them, a farewell lap, handed Uncle Padana my lamp, kicked past the brine pools and the spiked rocks and dead eels, mussels. No point in the lamplight, too deep. No point in eyes too deep. No point in explaining. No way of making sense of
    'Ta-ta.'
I tossed my chin over my shoulder and waved as I went over the edge. If I could pass on something, it would be to say that at the heart   at the heart   at the heart of things there is no sense. Sister. I brushed the tips of my fingers on the ledge of the seabed as they
    waved me off.

To Mum, Dad and Brother, for everything.

Acknowledgements

Thank you to the first readers and editors of this book, my cherished friends, talented writers Martin Wakefield, Kate Lockwood Jefford and Claire Montell.

To the many friends whose love and support, listening ears, readings and late night drinks have helped me along the way to publication.

To the Las Kellys movement, and the documentary *Hotel Explotación: Las Kellys*, directed by Georgina Cisquella, from which Noda's speech was adapted.

Thank you to my agent, Chris Wellbelove, and editor, Tamara Sampey-Jawad.

Part of this book was written and developed while I was in residence at the Amant Siena Residency, 2020.

Fitzcarraldo Editions
8-12 Creekside
London, SE8 3DX
United Kingdom

ISBN 978-1-913097-70-7

Design by Ray O'Meara
Typeset in Fitzcarraldo
Printed and bound by TJ Books

fitzcarraldoeditions.com

Fitzcarraldo Editions